Heroines of Avalon
and Other Tales

Also by Ayn Cates Sullivan, Ph.D.

Legends of the Grail: Stories of Celtic Goddesses

Three Days in the Light

The Windhorse: Poems of Illumination

Consider This: Recovering Harmony & Balance Naturally

Tracking the Deer: Early Poetry

Illustrated Fables for All Ages

Ella's Magic

A Story of Becoming

Sparkle & The Light

Sparkle & The Gift

Heroines of Avalon

and Other Tales

AYN CATES SULLIVAN, Ph.D.

Infinite Light Publishing
Santa Barbara, CA

Infinite Light Publishing
5142 Hollister Avenue, No. 115
Santa Barbara, CA 93111
www.infinitelightpublishing.com

First Edition

Library of Congress Control Number: PS3619.U42 H47 2018

Cataloging-in-Publication:

Names: Sullivan, Ayn Cates, author. | duCray, Belle Crow, illustrator.

Title: Heroines of Avalon / by Ayn Cates Sullivan ; illustrated by Belle Crow duCray.

Description: Santa Barbara, CA : Infinite Light Publishing, [2018] | Series: The Legends of the Grail series ; volume 2. | Includes bibliographical references and index.

Identifiers: ISBN: 978-1-947925-04-5 (hardback) | 978-1-947925-08-3 (paperback) | 978-1-947925-17-5 (eBook)

Subjects: LCSH: Mythology, British--Fiction. | Mythology, Celtic--Fiction. | Women, Celtic--Folklore. | Grail--Folklore. | Women--Folklore. | Women's studies. | Determination (Personality trait)--Fiction. | Self-actualization (Psychology)--Fiction. | Spirituality--Fiction. | LCGFT: Arthurian romances. | BISAC: FICTION / Visionary & Metaphysical. | FICTION / Fantasy / General. | SOCIAL SCIENCE / Women's Studies. | LITERARY COLLECTIONS / European / English, Irish, Scottish, Welsh.

Classification: LCC: PS3619.U42 H47 2018 | DDC: 813/.6--dc23

Summary: These stories are a collection of British myths and legends told in the traditional way with a twist. Each heroine tells her story in her own way, freeing herself of centuries of misunderstanding. This series of myths includes Dindraine, the only woman in Arthurian legend to achieve the Holy Grail. It is time to learn the names of the true Heroines of Avalon.

Illustrations: Belle Crow duCray
Editor: Robin Quinn
Cover Design: Lucinda Rae Kinch
Book Design: Ghislain Viau

These stories are dedicated to
Hannah May Hocking.
May the blessings of the Otherworld
always be with you!

Contents

II
Finding the Goddess in British Mythology
IOUGA & ELEN

III
Heroines of Avalon
ELAINE & DINDRAINE

DINDRAINE

Acknowledgments

From the Sky above
To the Earth below —
Thank you!

Writing a book of this nature requires a village. There are many people who have assisted me and deserve acknowledgment. I will name the inner circle, but know gratitude is extended to everyone who has helped bring this book into being. First of all, my husband, John Patrick Sullivan deserves a large kiss for being willing to embrace his inner King and fearlessly support me as the Celtic worlds open up for both of us. I wish to thank my children, Kathryn and William, for walking in sacred places and engaging in so many mystical experiences with open minds and hearts. Illustrator Belle Crow duCray has been willing to journey and dream with me and enter the Otherworlds to discover the faces of Goddesses, some of which had almost been forgotten. Thank you, Belle, for bringing these stories to life again for this generation. The journey is even more exciting with all of you.

Women who are attuned to the Goddesses like to look beautiful, so I want to thank makeup artist, photographer and colorist, Amber Sibley, who makes me feel comfortable in front of a camera. Thank you, Amber, for questing with me through all sorts of muddy fields and old roads looking for Goddesses and Heroines in the landscape, and carrying a bit of lipstick. Special gratitude is extended to Glastonbury bard Kieron Sibley for his bravery, wisdom, and his current understanding of the Ogham and the Celtic Wheel of Life.

Dr. Susan Lange listened gently to my body's wisdom with me during the writing of this book, and I wish to thank her for taking the time to write the Foreword. I want to acknowledge my brilliant editor Robin Quinn for polishing these tales and to Mcgovren Moore for carefully proofreading. Thank you to Ghislain Viau for taking the time to design these pages so carefully, and to Lucinda Rae for the beautiful cover design. Much gratitude must be extended to the late independent publishing expert Ellen Reid, who has crossed into the Otherworld, for encouraging me to believe in my own projects. Blessings and gratitude are extended to my mother, Gwendolyn Foster Cates, the true heroine of my life; and to my father, William Wesley Cates, who recently crossed like a King to the Blessed Isles and beyond.

I also want to thank a British healer, who wishes to remain nameless. By connecting me to the ancient mysteries and the light of the Divine, she changed my life in a very positive and life-affirming way forever. I am also grateful to the many healers and wisdom keepers who, out of fear of persecution, often do their work silently and generally for very little pay. I pray a time is emerging when we can explore what is presenting itself in our psyches without fearing persecution but with curiosity, intelligence and love.

I also want to thank scholar John Matthews for teaching me to journey in the tradition of Celtic Shamanism and for helping me embrace the idea that the Otherworlds are real. Further thanks to the hundreds of people who have joined me over the years in workshops, on the radio and on teleconferences. Together we can find our inner light. Together can make a difference! Most of all, thank you *Solas Siorai,* the Eternal Light, for showing me the way in each and every moment.

Foreword
Challenging Female Myths

According to Barbara Marx Hubbard, conscious evolutionary elder, now is a unique time in the history of our world. This is a special time where we get to consciously re-invent and re-create ourselves, to reclaim our power by facing our old shadows and wounds, to resolve old pain and suffering, and to transform our personal stories. We get to challenge the old female myths of martyrdom and self-sacrifice, so that we can transform our relationships with ourselves, with each other, with Mother Earth and the Divine Feminine. Read these stories of Goddesses and Heroines, so beautifully and respectfully recorded by Ayn Cates Sullivan, and illustrated by Belle Crow duCray, that help you drop into the deep archetypes of the Divine Feminine. Use these myths and legends to help tap into your own specific healing journey, to transform old patterns of struggle and suffering into your own unique and inspired story—the story of the emergence of your own gifts and dreams.

My Personal Connection

It is with great pleasure that I write this Foreword for Dr. Ayn Cates Sullivan, not only because of my own connection to Britain, but also because of my female lineage, through women very dear to my heart, whose legacies live on. Like Ayn Cates Sullivan, I have walked the lush lands of England, Ireland, Scotland and Wales, and connected deeply with the magical energies of that earth.

My mother-in-law, Detta Brigitta Lange, now in her nineties, taught workshops at the Chalice Well in Glastonbury, hosted women's circles, led vision quests on the moors, and was very connected to Findhorn and her circle garden. My mother, Jane, was called to move to South West England, close to Glastonbury, after a busy life in Southeast Asia, to nurture and self-heal in the rich years before she died. She was called there after reading books on the ancient teachings, and like Ayn, knew that she needed to re-connect deeply with the powerful healing energy of the Divine Feminine, held by Mother Earth.

The Written Word's Power to Heal

Ayn Cates Sullivan is masterful in weaving stories that heal as you read them, and this book is no exception. Just as my mother was called to move to the South West of Britain, the land of many of the legends in this book, for her own healing nearly 50 years ago, so you will find yourself called to go deep within as you read the words from this modern mystic. The time is now to deeply examine your own story and to get current with the incredible feminine power and wisdom that is available to us today as women, and also men. As women, we are invited to become our own heroines, to re-write our personal stories, to say, "Enough already. I now choose a different and more empowered vision!"

This is what I hope you take away from *Heroines of Avalon & Other Tales*, the personal awakenings of the Goddesses and Heroines who are telling their renewed stories through Ayn Cates Sullivan in these pages. If you suffer, dig deep and find the flawed programming. Surround yourself with empowering stories like the ones in this book, where the women—Goddesses and heroines like yourself—face untold obstacles, both inner and outer, and prevail. These are stories about women who become champions in their own lives, and then touch others. The stories are about women who can support their men in a more wholesome way.

These stories have global impact. We call on women everywhere to plumb their own depths, find their true, deep source of power, and emerge victorious, proud, healthy and free. When we are truly in balance and alive, our grail/wombs thrive and are connected directly with our hearts. Anything else is an indication that something is off. It means that we have lost our individual and collective connection with the power of the Divine Feminine. This is a power that we have been conditioned to disconnect from, to believe that we are separate from.

It's Time to Awaken

It is time to re-connect with the powerful lineage of the Divine Feminine. She is there for all. And as you re-connect with your own Holy Grail, you will find that the medicine of the ancient feminine is deeply healing, normal and natural. Your body knows exactly how to heal when you are connected to your womb and your heart. One of my favorite ancient Chinese proverbs is "When sleeping women wake, mountains move."

It's time for women worldwide to wake up and for mountains to move! It is time for our grails/wombs to wake up! It is with great joy and hope that I congratulate Dr. Ayn Cates Sullivan and welcome the new transformational re-telling of the legends of Goddesses and Heroines that she will introduce you to in these pages.

Susan Lange, O.M.D., L.Ac.
Doctor of Oriental Medicine
in Santa Monica, California
Author of *The 7 Toxic Lies: Break Through the Barriers of Family and Generational Trauma into the Magic of Your Own Core Light*

Introduction
A Vision by an Ancient Well

As a child, I knew that my true home was far away in a land that was green and magical. While growing up in Virginia, I heard stories about my ancestors who were from the British Isles. As the family story goes, the King of England gave our family a land grant. Although the land has been divided many times over the years, our family still owns a farm in Cumberland County. According to the Forrester family bible, the Foster bloodline links us to Robert the Bruce, King of the Scots, and stretches back through Ireland, the Ukraine and the Middle East to Enoch the Prophet. If we take the time to do ancestral research, each of us can discover an unbroken lineage of light.

I heard that my great-grandmother on my father's side was in the lineage of the Lloyds of London and that her ancestral line traces back to the royal Welsh Llewellyns. No wonder I am fascinated by Celtic myths and legends. From an early age, I knew that my ancestors were from the Celtic countries, including Great Britain, Ireland and also France.

In 1985, I was offered an overseas research award from King's College London to research the life and work of Lady Gregory, the woman behind the Irish Literary Renaissance. I was familiar with her contemporary, William Butler Yeats. Eager to earn my doctorate in Anglo-Irish Literature, I spent the next decade walking the British Isles, Ireland and France collecting myths and legends.

Stone Circles & Sacred Sites

After moving to London, I spent a decade visiting many sacred sites including Stonehenge and Avebury Stone Circles. Hundreds of people visit these sacred heritage sites and there are many stories about both places. I always liked the tale of Merlin conjuring up a great wind to carry the blue stones from Wales across the Bristol Channel to England, and the whispers of his apprentice Nimue. When we stand by the sacred stones of Stonehenge, Avebury, and other sacred sites, our imaginations are activated. There are some mystics who say that all we take with us when we cross to the Otherworlds is our imagination. There are practices at the end of each section that encourage the reader to journey into the Inner Worlds.

Pilgrimage to Glastonbury

Arriving into the town of Glastonbury, there is a remarkable sight. A bald hill carved with snaking lines etched into the soil is known as the Tor. The hill rises up and is crowned with a tower. There is something magnetic about the spot, and pilgrims from all over the world climb up the steep hill and marvel at the views of Somerset. Mystics claim that Glastonbury is the heart chakra of the world. If you take time to walk up the Tor and watch the sunset, you might have the sense that the Otherworlds are close.

Glastonbury is said to be the site of the earliest church in the West founded by Joseph, or Philip, or perhaps even the Magdalene, in the first century. It has been a place of spiritual pilgrimage for centuries and some, including the visionary poet William Blake, even considered it Britain's Jerusalem. Glastonbury is definitely a unique town with people from all walks of life. Before the arrival of Christianity, it was a place known to those who followed the ways of the Goddess, and it is still a Goddess stronghold. Anyone seeking the Goddesses can visit the Goddess Temple and Goddess House and learn about, even embrace, the Ladies of Avalon.

The stories of King Arthur and the Quest for the Holy Grail have always been amongst my favorite myths and legends. At the ruins of the Glastonbury Abbey, there is a chained off area with a marker near the high altar that is the legendary resting place of Arthur and his Queen, Guinevere. On my quest, I realized it was not only men who sought the mysterious Grail. Dindraine's story has been rescued here and retold. In the Vulgate Cycle, Dindraine is the first person to achieve the Holy Grail. If we look even more deeply, the Grail might be a symbol for the Goddess who disappeared with the arrival of Christianity. In some stories the Grail is the Magdalene, and for others the Grail is a Cauldron of Wisdom or Plenty.

The hillfort of Cadbury Castle is strongly associated with Camelot court, and is considered by some to be an energetic Grail Castle. I love the idea of a king who will ride out to rescue his people in a time of great need. There is an earlier British Goddess known as Artha, the eternal maiden who reminds us that life always renews itself. Perhaps it is Artha that we need to call now to restore the land.

I first visited Glastonbury over twenty-five years ago and it changed my life. The town is full of all sorts of people, and not all savory, but it seems to be a gathering place for all who feel the mystical pull of invisible realms. Some feel the call of the Tor and the legendary dragon that sleeps beneath it. Some do not know why they have been drawn to Glastonbury, yet know they have been changed in some way.

Gazing Across Somerset

For many years I made an annual pilgrimage to Glastonbury. Once, I remember walking in the rain along the narrow lanes and pathways simply feeling the energy of the living zodiac that is etched into the land of Somerset. I was imagining what standing on the dove of Aquarius might awaken inside of me. My rational mind denied that there was anything to the wild tales, but the mystic in me had to run to the top of the Tor no matter how heavy the downpour of rain. Arriving at the top of the Tor, I gazed across Somerset feeling as though I had stood there many times before.

On one particular visit, my daughter was a baby and I arrived struggling between the rationality of academia and more creative role of motherhood. I had spent years studying, but it seemed that the more I studied the more confused I became. I wanted to connect with my daughter in some way that was meaningful, but was not certain what that might look like. It seemed to me that the only solution was to find the archetypes of the feminine, the Heroines and Goddesses of the land. I wanted to undertake a Grail Quest.

It wasn't that I did not appreciate men. I had spent my entire life studying the ideas, philosophies, religions and the sciences handed to me by a predominately male culture. I had actually thrived at an Ivy League college and had embraced the western world as it had been taught. I was familiar with the stories of our patriarchy, but I started to feel that there were stories that had been lost. There were faint whispers and I had the sense that if I walked in contemplation by lakes, rivers and streams, just maybe I could start to remember the missing and untold stories of Britain. I needed a role model, and since there were few I could study, I decided to find out what a Goddess looked like.

Secrets of the Grail

The Chalice Well in Glastonbury is one of England's most ancient wells. Currently, the well is held in safe keeping by the Chalice Well Trust. It is set in a magnificent garden known for peace, healing and tranquility. For two thousand years, people have come to sip the red waters that flow through the healing gardens. Every religious and spiritual path is welcomed at the well, and I went to visit it too. I soon found myself with people who wore rosaries, as well as women who wore cloaks and left herbs as offerings. Mystics say that there is a lady of the well who can present herself to pure hearted seekers. Christians claimed that Joseph of Arimathea brought the Holy Grail (the cup that contained the blood of Christ) to England and that it was buried in the well. Others say it was where Mary Magdalene hid from enemies who denied that a woman could be the embodiment of the true church. Then there are more ancient stories of the healing women of Avalon and the mysterious Ladies of the Lake. Perhaps the priestesses of Avalon were initiated at the Chalice Well, or one like it, leaving their pasts behind and stepping into the role of true healers and seers. Perhaps veiled in time and mist, there is some truth to the legend that Joseph of Arimathea and his followers knew the true secret of the Grail and that the traces of an ancient lineage of Light is still hidden in the landscape of Somerset.

Vision at the Chalice Well

One morning, like many others, I sipped the cold water of the iron-rich, red spring that flows out of the Lion's head fountain in Chalice Well Gardens. That particular morning a Robin Redbreast landed beside me chirping, and I wondered if he had a message for me. I intuitively felt that my spiritual lion was awakening within, and purred as I walked down to the waterfall and healing baths, known as Arthur's Court. It is a place for cleansing and reflection. Taking off my shoes, I walked in the cold water. Tears flowed down my cheeks as I asked the spirits of the place to show me the Feminine Face of God. I slipped my wet feet back into my boots and made my way back to the Chalice Wellhead.

I walked around the well three times clockwise, which felt natural. I sat on the seat made of stone that circles the Chalice Well, and it rained just enough to clear the crowds. I did not mind that I was damp, because my tears matched the drops that fell on my green coat. I asked the well to send me a vision so that I could live with the fact that I was a woman. I focused on the Vesica Pisces on the well lid, and wondered if it was a symbol of the feminine, of heaven joining earth, or perhaps a place where we can walk between worlds.

As I wept, a feeling came over me, and I knew I must peer deeply into the dark waters of the well. An iron grid covers the well, but I leaned in on it and looked at the ferns and moss that grew inside the mouth of the well. I stared down into the darkness, and it seemed to me that my tears made it deep inside the earth.

I then sat back against the stone seat and closed my eyes. I must have fallen asleep, because a dream came to me in which a woman arose from the well. She shimmered in front of me, and then embraced me in a way I had never felt before. The Goddess was as vast as the nighttime sky, and in Her presence I felt that I was connected to a spiral of intelligence and love that knew no end.

"Look," she told me. I knew from my Judeo-Christian training that no one could look at the face of God and live, but I had to see Her face. What I saw was an ancient and luminous woman, who aged as I looked at her until she was old and silver-haired. She became a crescent moon, then a half moon, followed by a full moon that subsequently took the form of a child laughing and dancing. As I watched, the child became a maiden, and then an old woman, and then a moon once again. The face of the Goddess included all ages, all faces and eventually all people, all beings and all of creation.

When I awoke from my reverie, the smell of roses pervaded the garden. From that moment on I knew that the Goddess comes in many forms and has many faces. She embraces all ages, genders, races, all landscapes and all sentient beings. I realized my prayer had been answered. I had seen the face of the Goddess and had also discovered my expression within Her. The Goddess is the totality of existence, and we are part of Her. She has many faces, yet excludes no one and no thing. She is form and the formless. The Goddess is the Grail.

Quest for the Holy Grail

Recently I discovered through DNA testing that my family is related to the most powerful woman of the 12th century. Eleanor of Aquitaine (1122-1204), the daughter and heiress of William, Duke of Aquitaine and Count of Poitiers, possessed more land than the French King. After inheriting her father's land, Eleanor married Louis VII of France and rode with him on the Second Crusade to protect the kingdom of Jerusalem. Eleanor fell in love with the stories of King Arthur and the Quest for the Holy Grail. After her marriage with Louis was annulled, she married Henry II, King of England. It is hard to know how accurate DNA testing is, especially with grandmothers of previous centuries. However, I can imagine Eleanor astride her horse with a silver saddle and a hawk on her wrist riding toward Jerusalem, her mind focused on achieving the Holy Grail.

If it is true that time is not linear but spiral, even now Eleanor is determined to reach the Holy Land and find the spark of light that resides in all that is good and true. We can ride with Eleanor through the mists of time and return changed. After her quest, Eleanor became the most powerful woman of her era.

Today, I feel Queen Eleanor smile upon us, inviting us to take the greatest journey of them all. Saddle up your favorite horse, and call the bird of your choosing. Together we will travel to a land that is far and yet no further away than that of your own imagination. Come with me and meet the heroines who achieved the Grail, and the Goddesses who guard an even more ancient power.

I
Finding the Goddess in Welsh Mythology

ARIANRHOD & BLODEUWEDD

ARIANRHOD

(pronounced "ahr-ee-AHN-hrod")

Arianrhod In Welsh Mythology

Mother Goddess & Enchantress

Arianrhod is a Celtic Moon Mother Goddess who is the ruler of Caer Sidi, an enchanted island located off the coast of Wales. Caer Sidi is sometimes seen as a revolving castle or a portal to Annwn, a Celtic Otherworld. In folklore, Arianrhod rides her celestial chariot through the sky as she observes the tides. She oversees who is coming into the world and who is departing. Arianrhod is the archetypal womb Goddess who connects us to birth, death and re-birth. Her Silver Wheel is a symbol of reincarnation.

Arianrhod plays an important role in the fourth branch of the Welsh 14th century *Mabinogion*. This collection of Welsh stories, although written after Christianization, narrates an earlier history of Wales that gives us a glimpse of a more ancient past. The stories were meant for bards in training, and they concern the children of the Goddess Don, similar to the Irish Mother Goddess Danu. The stories of the daughters of Don suggest that there was a matrilineal culture, which tracked descendants through the mother and not the father.

Commonly in many ancient myths and legends, members of the same family (including sisters and brothers) often marry or become lovers and produce children. In Arianrhod's tale, she has a special, intimate relationship with her brother/lover Gwydion. Clearly there is a taboo on the intermarrying of family members in the human world (or Middle Earth), but you will discover that most Celtic Gods and Goddesses arise out of the same source and that in some way we are all one great family. In the Otherworlds we can have many intimate connections.

The fourth branch of the *Mabinogion* tells the tale of the seduction or rape of Goewin, who was the ceremonial foot-holder of the shadowy King Math of Gwynnedd (Math fab Mathonwy). Due to a Celtic *geis* or taboo that had been placed on the monarch, the foot-holder of King Math had to be a virgin. Arianhrod was chosen as Goewin's successor. Before she could take the position, Arianhrod had to prove her virginity.

Arianrhod's mixed reputation in Wales is due to the custom of mothers being required to give their children names and weapons— and she refused her children both, until tricked by Gwydion, her brother/lover. Arianrhod is mother of both light (Lleu) and darkness (Dylan). She has been compared with the Greek Ariadne, Goddess of Mazes and Labyrinths, for she teaches us to always live at the center of existence.

Arianrhod embodies the magic of forgiveness, and she shows us how to live again after we have fallen. She is sometimes referred to as one of the three white ladies of Britain, perhaps because her essence can never be tainted by the words or deeds of others. Even though Arianrhod was betrayed, she learned to love again. She can help us let go of the suffering that no longer serves us. We can all learn to forgive, for that balances the light and the darkness within our hearts, freeing our souls. It is said that she flies through the night with her Silver Wheel bringing threads of comfort to those who seek her.

If you go outside at night and look with your inner eye, you might see her moving between stars, sometimes in the form of a white owl. Or you might find Arianrhod in the form of moonbeams dancing on a moving sea. If you go out tonight and listen to the whispers between stars, you might see her riding her pale chariot across the sky even now.

Arianrhod's Untold Story

The Greatest Test

Arianrhod lived on a sea-kissed, Otherworldly island known as Caer Sidi. Her maidens had covered the island in silver stars, so that only the wisest seers could find their way to her. Usually there was not much need for Arianrhod to come to the surface lands. Still, the salt of the sea air interlocked the Goddess's hair with sea flowers, so that she looked and felt like a mermaid, and usually she swam to the stars. For centuries, only the birds could find her, as well as her brother, Gwydion, whom she loved.

After Gwydion grew up to be a man, he spent much of his time in the Otherworld known as Annwn, for he was attracted to its sweet intoxications. His darker nature, however, would eventually draw him to stir up trouble in the world of the shady King Mathonwy of Gwynnedd, which is where our tale begins.

Whenever Gwydion came to visit his sister Arianrhod, they would remember their childhood and skip across the waves like silver

19

flying-fish. Sometimes they would ride dolphins, which enjoyed their play. No one knew about the symphonies they created, except the wind, who tends to share secrets.

Their play attracted curious elementals who were interested in Arianrhod's Silver Wheel and how she wove the songs of the earth into the fabric of existence. She did not see the harm of sharing the work with them, and taught the nature spirits to thread light. She showed them how to weave colour* and sound to create the fabric from which all of life arises. Arianrhod thought that would satisfy them, but it just attracted more who wanted to sit with her and learn.

Arianrhod lived with 13 white owls that hovered in the skyline at sunset. There they would catch the rays of the stars in their talons in order to focus their cosmic light. She taught the elementals that the music of the spheres affects the way flowers blossom. The pulse of the planets also impacts a person's soul blueprint and how one lives into it.

The undines and other water spirits loved creating mist, and some played with the patterns of morning frost, which curled like vines on the rocky shore. The sacred stones stirred to life and began to send out one pulse of love a day in alignment with the heartbeat of the Great Mother Goddess. Life was so attuned in those times, and Arianrhod delighted in teaching spirits and her gathering students how to work harmoniously with one another. Soon the island was covered in flowers, vines and broad-leafed ferns. The flora attracted birds in droves, adding to the island's sacred symphony.

---

* The British spelling of colour is used in this book in honor of the culture.

Yet all things change. The moon wove her light around the Silver Wheel and the tides turned, the age of peace fading into a new dawn. The water became increasingly shallow, and Gwydion returned to disturb Arianrhod's harmony. Gods and Goddesses enjoy exploring the many delights of life together, but this time her brother requested something that Arianrhod refused. Oh, how he pleaded. You have to understand that Gwydion is one of the children of the fertile Goddess Don, who sprang from a deep well on the ocean floor. He shared the Goddess's radiance and knew how to use magic to ensnare his sister in a web.

The day he arrived, Arianrhod was tending the sacred stones and flowers on the south slope of the isle. Gwydion looked at her with his deep sapphire-blue eyes, as a little wisp of blond hair began to curl on his forehead from the sea's mist. She knew her brother was motivated by some deep desire, but allowed him to twirl the sunlight around her ankles.

"Our Uncle Math needs a new virgin to hold his feet," he told her.

Arianrhod continued helping the ferns and flowers unfurl, and then she played with the shapes in the swirling mist. Gwydion had brought her a new wand, and although she did not really need his magic, she was enjoying the feel of the beautifully carved oakwood in her hand.

"What happened to the other foot-holder?" asked Arianrhod.

"Her name is Goewin. Uncle Math has married her," he answered.

Arianrhod thought there was probably much more to this story than Gwydion was sharing. "Why would he do that and risk breaking his *geis*?" she questioned. "Won't he lose his magic if his feet touch the ground?"

"Actually, he would die," Gwydion clarified.

"Goewin must be a beautiful queen," Arianrhod said, beginning to feel that her brother wished to draw her in further to this tale. "And I have not been invited to the wedding."

"Oh yes you have," countered Gwydion, who pulled her to him. Arianrhod danced with him and laughed.

"Let's go together," he said to his sister, who could see that Gwydion was drawing a golden thread in her mind down the path to the castle of King Math.

Arianrhod hesitated, intuiting that she was being tricked into more than her brother was communicating. Gwydion did tend to get into mischief, and she was not particularly fond of her dark uncle.

"You go and tell me about the wedding afterward," Arianrhod said, turning back to tending her island.

"You really must come with me," Gwydion insisted.

Arianrhod noticed that his voice had faltered and her brother was looking away as if concerned.

"What did you do?" she asked, sensing the need to know further details.

"Well, you see Goewin is very beautiful," began Gwydion, turning a little pink.

She loved that as naughty as Gwydion could be, his heart was still pure and he knew when he had strayed.

"Do you love her?" Arianrhod guessed.

"No, it's our brother Gil," he explained.

"Gilfaethwy fell in love with Goewin?" she reiterated. "That's marvelous, because he usually just takes what he wants."

"Gil tried to woo her. He really did," Gwydion replied defensively. "I watched him! He sang love songs to her, showed Goewin how flowers sprout from seeds, and how the sun can make the dew sparkle on the trees at night. He even brought a dress back from Annwn, but she still refused him."

"The poor girl probably knew that Math would kill her if she was not fit for the job of virgin foot-holder," she reasoned. She then looked sharply at Gwydion, and scolded, "Gilfaethwy knows better."

"Sometimes for a man the desire becomes so strong that he simply must possess a woman," he excused.

"So he raped her?" Arianrhod asked.

"Well, I arranged a meeting for them," he said.

"And then he took her," she speculated.

"It wasn't completely against her will," Gwydion said oversensitively.

Arianrhod closed her eyes and viewed the scene with her inner vision. Her violent brother Gilfaethwy had thrown the maiden to the ground and stolen her virginity from her. He had quickly run back to Annwn when he was finished. Arianrhod saw Goewin's torn dress and forlorn look, as she realized her job had been taken and probably her life as well.

Gwydion told Arianrhod that when King Math had called for Goewin the next morning, she had not come. So the King had sent his people to find her. The maiden had not wanted to go to him in her current state, but his majesty had responded in a way she had not expected. He asked for water to be drawn and heated, and for a bath with cleansing herbs to be prepared for her.

"Uncle Math loves her," Arianrhod said. "That is unlike him. And Gil deserves to be punished, and so do you for helping him commit an act of violence."

"I thought they would have a bit of fun," claimed Gwydion, now completely red-faced and ashamed.

Arianrhod felt anger rising up within her and the wind began to howl. "You wrecked her life," she said with disgust.

"I have been punished already," Gwydion informed her. "For three years, while Math has been engaged in battles, Gil and I have been under enchantment. I have learned that the feminine must be honored."

"Who punished you?" she asked. "Mathonwy cursed you, no doubt?"

"Math was so furious that he turned Gil and me into a doe and stag." He blushed again and began to wring his hands.

"You and our brother didn't mate, did you?" she teased. Seeing the answer on Gwydion's face, Arianrhod started to laugh. "You and Gil?"

"It's not funny," Gwydion told her. "I couldn't contain myself. As a stag, there was nothing in my mind but lust, eating and fighting. Not necessarily in that order."

"How long did the enchantment last?"

"A year."

"That's not too bad for an immortal," she said, patting his arm. But Gwydion threw his arms around her waist and began to sob.

"Math turned us into a boar and a sow next!"

"Get off!" she protested, using her Light to cast him backwards. "So you mated with our brother once again? Poor Gil." Now she was doubling over with laughter.

"It isn't funny," objected Gwydion. "I was the sow that time."

Arianrhod squealed with laughter and chased him around making pig noises. "Was the sex good?" she taunted.

"Vicious," he said, grabbing her chin. But she slapped his hand away.

"It seems that you would have learned to honor the feminine by now," Arianrhod noted, then grew to her full height of 13 feet. She turned her back to her brother, caught rays of Light in her hands, and began to sing. Her maidens with silver sparkles in their hair came to assist her.

"I love and honor the Goddess!" he declared, looking up at Arianrhod with pure devotion.

"So what happened in the third year of your punishment?" Arianrhod asked, as she cloaked her island in mist.

"Math turned us into a pair of wolves." Gwydion bared his teeth at his sister. "Gil was the she-wolf," he added with a howl.

"Has he released you from your animal bonds and forgiven you and Gil now?" she inquired, knowing that her Uncle Math did not have that sort of reputation.

"There is one condition," he revealed, coming close to Arianrhod and taking her hands. He looked up at her with some hesitation.

"No," Arianrhod told him, before he asked. "Do not trick me like you do others."

"Listen, he is going to turn us into a rooster and a hen next, unless I find a virgin to hold his feet."

Arianrhod made chicken noises, but then saw that her brother had started to cry. She sat down beside Gwydion and stroked his hair. He seemed so very sad, and she did have the sense that his well-earned punishment had done its work. He had learned his lesson, although she wondered if that were true for violent Gilfaethwy.

"What would I have to do?" Arianrhod asked.

"Our uncle needs a new foot-holder," he said. "When he is not engaged in battle, a virgin must keep his channel of magic open. He has a *geis* that has been placed on him, and without the pure feminine holding his feet, his powers start to diminish."

"Men should learn how to attune to the earth standing on their own two feet," replied Arianrhod sternly. "If he needs a virginal maid, you need to look elsewhere."

"A king must connect to the spirit of the land through a woman. Virgin means open channel of creation, and you are that," replied Gwydion. "There is no other way."

Arianrhod took a deep breath because she knew that the land's abundance depended upon the sacred union of the King and the Queen. She did not wish a famine or plague on anyone. Looking at her misty home, she decided that it might be time to have an adventure in the world of men. So she chose to follow her brother in the silvery light of the full moon to the home of King Mathonwy.

King Math's castle was much darker than the Goddess had remembered. Arianrhod shivered as she walked with Gwydion through a hall lined with open-mouthed gargoyles. She saw Goewin off in the distance, recognizing her from the visions. Before Arianrhod and Gwydion could get close to her, the pale girl hurried down a passageway and out of sight. Arianrhod wondered what had really happened to Goewin and if she were happy in her role as the King's wife.

"Don't look so downhearted," said Gwydion, giving Arianrhod a peck on the cheek. "He's not as scary as all that."

"I hope his feet don't smell," Arianrhod grumbled. "If they do, I won't hold them."

"If they do, then wash them in rosewater and he will love you forever," suggested her brother.

"That's what I'm afraid of," Arianrhod sighed. Brightening, she added, "I already have your love, which is quite enough."

Gwydion blushed slightly, took her hand, and walked with his head held high into King Math's throne room.

As the brother and sister arrived at Math fab Mathonwy's court, Arianrhod noticed a darkness that appeared to hover over the heavy wooden furniture and dusty tapestries. Thick candles burned between large gemstones and old manuscripts. Arianrhod watched as red wax dripped onto the floor. Two hounds looked at her with indifference.

Then the King turned his grizzled face in the direction of the Goddess. Gwydion felt himself flinch. Math watched his pretty niece approach, and he smiled hungrily. His black eyes were full of deceit and trickery, yet at the same time there was something seductive about him. When Arianrhod walked closer, Math provocatively grabbed her skirt, perhaps searching for something more flesh-like. She slapped his hand away and he winced, losing his smile.

"I told you she is pure," said Gwydion. "And best left that way."

Math snorted and clanged his copper plate. His servants and dogs all came running. "I'm hungry," he declared. "And give this wench some meat also."

Arianrhod thought her uncle was quite disgusting, and she would have left, but Gwydion grabbed her hand. "Just until we find another suitable foot-holder," he whispered. "Do it for Gil's sake."

"Goddesses don't sacrifice themselves for others," she pointed out in a hushed tone. "But I will do it so the land does not despair, and to keep the balance between light and darkness. But when spring comes, I will return home."

Math was studying his niece, and he uttered to Gwydion, "She doesn't like me, and I don't trust her. It looks like you two like each other too much." He smiled at Gwydion and winked.

Arianrhod began to feel ill, and she prayed that the Great Goddess might relieve her of this tedious work before it even began.

"You have to prove you're a virgin before you can hold my sacred feet," Math commanded. His feet looked white and cold, with blue toenails that twisted into points. Even from where she stood, Arianrhod knew that they smelled like a rutting goat.

She looked at Gwydion, who pleaded with large blue eyes. "What would the test be that I need to pass?" Arianrhod asked, after glancing back to the King.

"I wouldn't want to grow ill just because you and your brother decided that my throne would fit you both." Math grinned and held up his wand. She had heard of his magic, and knew also that it was not always white.

"Perhaps you would rather find another foot-holder," she said haughtily. "Someone who fits your needs more exactly." She cupped her hands under her breasts just to taunt him. Her behavior seemed to anger the King, but Arianrhod was beginning to have fun with the sorcerer, who seemed to believe that his magic might be stronger than her own.

"If you're a virgin, then step over my wand," he directed, holding his wand erectly in his lap.

"It might be difficult," she replied. "Your throne is rather high."

"And you are a Goddess," he reminded her. "So perhaps you could spin a silver thread and fly over me."

"So you can look up my skirts?" she asked, no longer amused.

"Call in Gilfaethwy so I can order his execution," said King Math loudly.

Arianrhod watched the King's men leave the court to go drag her guilty brother from his dungeon. They heard Gil scream, and then her brother was dragged in and thrown before Math's throne. As shamefaced as Gilfaethwy might be, he was still her brother. His clothes were torn, his skin looked grey, and his eyes were downcast. Gilfaethwy had been defeated by Math and the punishment had gone on long enough.

In that moment, Arianrhod decided that she must do her best to help her brother. Gilfaethwy was the one who needed to learn the ways of the Goddess, but it was more likely that he would learn if he were alive.

Arianrhod rose to her full height of 13 feet, cast a glamor around herself, and began to flirt with the King to win his affections.

"Release Gilfaethwy and I will show you what Goddesses are made of."

King Math laughed, amused by her game, and nodded to his soldiers who roughly released the young man. Without a word, Gilfaethwy turn and fled. Arianrhod listened as his footsteps faded until they could no longer be heard. Sensing that Gil had escaped the walls of the fortress, she turned her focus to King Math and her new assignment. A Goddess always has the choice to appear ugly or beautiful, and in this moment, she was radiant. A luminosity appeared around her and Math winced as if burned by Arianrhod.

"You must pass the test!" he roared.

In response to his demand, she cast a silver thread from her left palm and another from her right.

Math fab Mathonwy's smile broadened. "Jump, I dare you," he taunted.

"Hold up your wand!" she said, swinging as gracefully as a spider over his throne.

What Arianrhod did not realize was that Math had heard rumors of the Goddess's love for mermen as well as her brother, and he had laid a trap for her. The King used his magic to still Arianrhod's movement so that she rested helplessly above him. Light shot up from his wand and she felt a gush in her womb. Arianrhod cried out and kicked until she was beyond the King's grasp, but her womb continued to cramp. Tumbling to the cold floor, she felt a sudden and surprising pain. Breathing heavily, she had no choice but to accept the flow of life that was moving through her body.

"Don, Mother Goddess help me," she murmured, growing faint from shock and the intensity of the moment. She gave a yell loud enough to shake the stone foundation of the fortress.

Dylan came first, the son of the sea. Her dark son was born a strong youth, and he knew to run to his watery home beneath the waves. Dylan left before anyone could snare him, but he was not the end of Arianrhod's labor. Another ball of flesh slid from her womb, and it was not the child's time to be born. However, before Arianrhod could respond to this horror, Gwydion took the form and placed it in a wooden chest.

The King roared with laughter but Arianrhod had become enraged by his trickery. Blood staining her dress, she pulled herself up from the floor and stood with her hand on a stone pillar for strength.

"I curse you Math fab Mathonwy to the shadows of ghouls and the cold of loneliness!" said Arianrhod with wrath. "And as for this last creature of magic, may it never find a name, weapon or any wife."

Gwydion cared for the child in the chest, wrapping it in blankets and creating a womb out of words that he chanted—protecting the baby from its wrathful mother.

"Was that the plan all along?" she demanded of Gwydion. "Men cannot give birth, and so they force the Goddess. But when it is against her will, it tends not to go so well."

She meant to kill the baby, but Gwydion stopped her.

"No, sister, leave the child with me," he said.

She looked down at the baby and then back at her brother. "It might come from my womb, but it isn't of me."

"All children are of the Goddess," he countered.

"Enjoy being a mother sow," Arianrhod hissed. "I hope you grow tits!"

Pulling her cloak around her, Arianrhod exited the court. As she left, the room became icy and the candles went out. Math laughed and ordered his men to re-light the flames.

The moon hid as Arianrhod flew back to her island, swearing that it was the last time she would engage in the world of men.

From then on when Gwydion came to see her, Arianrhod refused him. One of her maidens told the Goddess that the second child had been raised in a magical chest. The maiden added that in order for the child to make his way in the world, Arianrhod needed to give him a name. Arianrhod said he was no son of hers, but of Math's dark magic. Just the thought of seeing the child filled her with such outrage that she rejected him as her own.

Years went by, and Arianrhod put the world of men out of her mind. She began to enjoy her misty island Caer Sidi once again, where food was abundant and life was everlasting. Hoping that all men would forget of her existence, Arianrhod blended her island with the waves of the sea and the stones they crashed against. Only maidens were allowed to be in Arianrhod's presence, and she tended to shun all children.

One particular day, when the sun had just coaxed the opening of some yellow flowers that grow at the edge of the sea, Arianrhod heard laughter. She turned around to see what appeared to be a sunbeam touching the silver strands of her wheel. Looking more closely, she observed a child naturally weaving Light with his hands to enhance life. Arianrhod was delighted and laughed. "Lleu Llaw Gyffes," she said, "you of the radiant light certainly have skillful hands."

Gwydion stepped forward and said, "This is our son, and even though you swore you never would, you have given him his name—Lleu Llaw Gyffes, bright one of the skillful hands."

"Get out of here before I set my owls on you!" Arianrhod yelled at Gwydion and her son, who lowered his bright gaze. She looked at the boy for a moment and noticed that his hair had the same golden curls as her brother.

The white owls began to gather and glared with eerie yellow eyes down at the males. Gwydion did not flee but looked at her squarely and asserted, "This child was unformed but I saved him. He was born out of my love for you. I raised him as ours, and I hope that one day you can welcome him into your heart."

"There is no room in my heart for men!" Arianrhod shouted, unleashing her white owls.

The owls spread their wings, casting a wintry shadow as they chased the two visitors back into their boat and across the Irish sea to the Math's castle.

Several more years passed, and Arianrhod occasionally thought about her brother and son, but it was still mostly with contempt. When focusing on it too much, she caused storms to form that blew down the largest oaks. The elementals would come and ask her to please stop, because the branches and leaves were being broken and scattered. To try to prevent another visit by Gwydion, the white owls patrolled her shores.

After a great while, Arianrhod tried to find forgiveness in her heart. She knew that King Math was being the shadowy old trickster he had always been. It was Gwydion who she could not forgive, because she had trusted and loved him. She felt he was the one who had truly betrayed her.

When Lleu had grown, Gwydion returned with the young man to Arianrhod's island once again. This time, Arianrhod allowed them to enter her world, but kept her owls close by.

"You must give your son his weapon if he is to become a man," said Gwydion.

"What became of Gil?" asked Arianrhod.

"Uncle Math captured him and made him a pig herder, but eventually forgave him. He is less cruel than you," answered her brother sadly.

"Lleu is not my son, and a Goddess never forgets a betrayal," she told Gwydion. "Go, before I set my owls loose on you again."

A moment later, her maidens rushed in with the news that there was an attack on the island. Arianrhod looked outside and saw ships on the horizon. She opened the door of her armory and quickly handed each person nearby a sword. As the vision of the ships began to fade, Arianrhod realized that Gwydion and Lleu both were bearing arms, and that Gwydion had fooled her with a mirage.

"Thank you for giving your son a weapon," said Gwydion, who leaned against a standing stone and wore a broad grin on his face.

"Never will I trust you again!" roared Arianrhod, releasing her owls, which bore down on the two men tearing their hair and clothing. "And I place a curse on Lleu that he will never have a wife born of a woman!"

But Gwydion and Lleu were as quick as sunlight and slipped out of sight without a trace.

Arianrhod built a fortress around her island and asked her priestesses to keep watch. No men were allowed inside her sacred temple, and those who attempted entry were treated harshly.

Many years went by, and Arianrhod slowly forgot about the trickery of the human world. Instead, love and compassion filled her heart once again.

One day a shoemaker came to measure the priestesses for their winter boots. Arianrhod was distracted that day and did not notice that it was a man who held her feet. When she looked down, Gwydion removed his hat and sat back looking up at her. As she looked at his lined face and open gaze, Arianrhod realized that she no longer hated her brother. In fact, she had created a barrier to the very man she loved. Smiling, she spun a web of Light around him.

"I'm very sorry that you felt betrayed," said Gwydion, looking up at her meekly. "I am also learning."

Arianrhod frowned from being reminded of the betrayal and wanted to screech at him like one of her owls. But the years on the island had mellowed her, and tears began to run down her cheeks.

"Why did you trick me?" she asked tearfully.

"I did not mean to trick you," responded Gwydion truthfully. "I didn't know that Math would test you in such a way. I thought virgin meant open channel. After all, isn't that the role of the Goddess? Please forgive me."

"Definitions change over time," said Arianrhod. "You knew of our love, which was enough to make me unfit for the position. Why do men always need to test a woman's purity? Don't you know that an embodied Goddess is what brings you pleasure?"

"I do now," Gwydion told her. "I still love you."

Arianrhod looked at him long and hard. A tear trickled down her left cheek. Finally she professed, "I have had enough of pain and sorrow. I forgive you and please forgive me."

Gwydion reached up and took her hand. "I promise never to betray you again, but to honor you as I always should have."

"We will see if you can keep your promise," replied Arianrhod, who noticed that her heart felt lighter than it had in decades. "And since we are celebrating, I will offer Lleu a gift."

"A wife?" asked Gwydion. "He pines for a woman."

"A woman he will never have," she said, "because I would never put a woman through the sort of agony that you have both torn my soul with."

"But I thought I had been forgiven," protested Gwydion. "And surely our son is worthy of more than just your rejection."

"Later this spring, please bring me some freshly picked wildflowers," she said smiling, "and I will show you what I will make for Lleu."

One spring morning, Lleu knelt in front of his mother, Goddess Arianrhod of the Silver Wheel.

"Lleu," she said, "you came to me as a surprise. I am now glad your father raised you in a chest so that you could step fully into your manhood. I swore I would not gift you with a name or weapons, and yet the Goddess bestowed them upon you. As for a wife, we shall see."

"Thank you, Goddess," said Lleu. "I now have what it takes to lead my own life and I feel the quest calling me. Thank you."

He smiled at his parents, then whistled for his winged horse. Arianrhod and Gwydion watched as their son rode toward the morning sun with deliberation and speed, across the Irish sea, and through a portal to the mainland. He did not look back.

All the years of suffering vanished, and Arianrhod realized there was no need to reject the ones she actually loved. Arianrhod walked over to Gwydion and said to him, "Come, let's swim and see if we can find the Old Man of the Sea and his son Dylan. There might be more forgiveness to make under the waves."

Soon Gwydion and Arianrhod had turned into silver Merfolk who leapt in joy in the waves. And perhaps they found Dylan in Tir fa Tonn, the Land Under Waves.

Honoring the Goddess Arianrhod

Celebrating Arianrhod
The Silver Circle

The most magical of Don/Danu's children, Arianrhod is celebrated on December 2. Her Silver Circle, Star or Wheel is said to be where souls await the time of their birth. Arianrhod is often seen as the ancestral guardian that holds the gate of the north. To bring more meaning into the winter holiday season, a silver circle or star can adorn your home to remind you of your eternal connection to your ancestors. This wise and powerful matriarch knows when it is correct for you to step into your power, and also when to relinquish it. For more information on the Eightfold Calendar of the Year: The Celtic Wheel of Life, see the appendix at the back of the book.

Celebrating the Shining Ones

The correct order of the universe is as clear to Arianrhod as the rising and setting of the sun and the many phases of the moon, which combine to create her sacred Silver Circle. Arianrhod gives birth to the God of Light, Lleu, known for the brightness of his face and multiple talents.

Lleu is celebrated during the summer harvest festival on or around August 1 known as Lughnasadh or Lammas. This is a time to remember the challenges we have faced and overcome, a day to feast in the name of the shining ones. Arianrhod and her family can also be celebrated during Lughnasadh.

Arianrhod In Nature
Owls, Mermaids & The Spirits of Birch Trees

Arianrhod is loved by all designs of creation, including all flowers for she knows their medicine intimately. Arianrhod's bird is the Owl. We may also find Arianrhod whispering through the cry of a Seabird, or in the form of a Mermaid swimming silently in the Irish or Celtic Sea. On certain days when the mist clears off the coast of Wales and the sun shines at just the right angle, you might be able to see Caer Sidi, her enchanted island.

Birch Trees

Arianrhod's favorite tree is the pale and slender Birch, with its heart-shaped leaves and white or silver paper-thin bark that sheds each year like a silver snake. After the Ice Age, the Birch was one of the first trees to grow in Ireland and Britain, and soon songbirds filled their branches. Because of its long existence and connection to the Goddess, the Birch tree has an ancient and magical history. The earliest Celtic writing is known as the Ogham, and the Beithe or Birch is used to etch the first symbol of this ancient alphabet. Like Arianrhod, Birch teaches us about renewal, rebirth and new beginnings.

Birch Ogham

39

The Birch tree is also amongst the first in the forest to show its leaves in the spring. Mothers intuitively place Birch leaves and bark around their babies to protect them from negativity. Perhaps in memory of the Ice Age, each year during December and January those of the Goddess tradition take rods made of Birch (Birch wands) and drive out the spirits of winter.

In Wales, Birch wreaths were woven as tokens of love, and the tree's trunk is sometimes used for Maypole dancing. It may be that the silver spirits of these trees reside in Caer Sidi with Arianrhod.

As an essence, the Birch helps us overcome worry and anxiety, instead freeing the imagination so situations can be seen from all perspectives. When a breeze blows through a forest of Birch trees, there is often a gentle melody that sweeps negativity away, healing our hearts and souls. If you listen carefully, you might hear Arianrhod and the mermaids of Caer Sidi making music that encourages all things to thrive and grow.

Arianrhod's Colours
Silver, Yellow & Violet

Arianrhod's three sacred colours — Silver, Yellow and Violet — help her weave the web of life. Arianrhod sometimes wears a Violet cloak with Silver wheels, Yellow stars and crescent Moons, in honor of her deep magic.

Silver is the colour of the thread or Star Line that keeps us linked to our personal essence and ultimately to the Source of eternal existence. Silver is an important color to use when we want to understand where we fit in the universe. Violet is the colour of healing and all things spiritual. Silver and Violet are magical colours that support Arianrhod in living in alignment with the principles that form the universe. The colour Yellow is linked with intelligence, as well as personal joy and brilliancy. Her combination is known as "Pure Magic."

"Pure Magic"

Meeting the Goddess Arianrhod

Each person living on Earth has a unique connection to the spiritual world. The energy that connects us is called the Star Line, and it is often seen as a silver thread of Light that leads us back to our origin. As our Higher Self, we are Light Beings. Yet when we are born into the world, we enter a veil of forgetfulness.

It is time to call upon Arianrhod when we are ready to cut through the illusion of separation and align with our spiritual nature. The pure magic of Arianrhod links us back to our original Light. Don or Danu, the mother of Arianrhod, tends our thread until it is time for us to return to her Cosmic lap. You will know she is with you, because you will feel a subtle tug at the nape of your neck. You may also be aware of the Light that shines from your fingertips.

Practice 1
Locating the Silver Thread

If you wish to remember your spiritual connection and feel the Light of your eternal self, locate your etheric Silver Thread. This takes some ingenuity and sensitivity to discover. Generally located in the hollow of the back of your neck just above the atlas/axis of the spine, there you will discover an etheric Silver Thread. When you touch it, you may feel lightness, as if there is a part of you that already knows how to fly. When you have located it successfully, you may feel as though your body has been charged by a cosmic battery. Once you are fully aligned with your Light, you may also be more fully aware of your innate gift to heal with light, colour and sound.

Every night during sleep, we return to our Star to be healed and nourished. If we call upon her, Arianrhod can collect us in her chariot drawn by owls, and we can consciously follow our Silver Thread back to our original Star.

Practice 2
Whispering Between Worlds

If you need to speak to a loved one – such as a well-loved grandparent who has crossed on to the Otherworld – ask your Higher Self if you can access their Silver Thread. It is a deeply nurturing exercise for both parties, because you can be reminded that in Spirit there is no separation.

You can use Silver Threads the same way you use telephone wires when you make a call on a telephone. The lines are already installed, all we have to do is use the spiritual connections that already exist. You may or may not hear their voice, but you can always leave a message. Prayers and blessings are always heard. Sometimes you will simply have a feeling or a flash of insight about how a loved one is doing in their new life. Do not doubt it, but simply hold the thought or feeling in your heart.

The Celtics knew that our friends and family live on, and that one day we will join them in celebration again. It is possible to stay in relationship with people long after they have left our human world. This is useful because we know who to call when it is our time to step into the Tunnel of Light and cross on to the next dimension. Arianrhod is one of the guides who can lead you through the northern gate back to your spiritual home. We are and will be held and cared for forever.

Visualization
Threads of Starlight

When preparing for your visualizations, create a quiet and meditative space where you will not be disturbed. It is the silver birch that opens up the way for those new to journeying. In Celtic drawings, you will often see a never-ending line showing how the beak of a bird may become part of a tree that will then flow into the form of a fish. The idea is that all things are connected. As you practice these visualizations and get more accustomed to traveling into the Otherworlds, you may discover that you also begin to shape-shift. Close your eyes, and take three deep breaths. It is time to travel to the Otherworldly spinning island known as Caer Sidi.

Rise up in your spirit body and notice that your physical body is below you safely guarded by Arianrhod. She is calling for you, and soon you notice that a large silver circle in the shape of a flying carpet is in front of you waiting for you to climb onboard. Sitting upon the circle, you immediately notice that you feel safe. Arianrhod's silver circle knows exactly where to take you.

You travel quickly out over the ocean, and then you are surprised when the silver circle takes you below the water. In the Otherworlds you can breathe underwater. Sliding off the silver circle, you realize with delight that you can move as quickly as a dolphin. Silvery fish swim beside you encouraging you to jump and play. A mermaid comes to join you, and smiling, she invites you to swim with her to

Caer Sidi, the home of Arianrhod. Respect is key in the Otherworld and as soon as you arrive, you thank the mermaid for acting as a trustworthy guide. Immediately, the veils to the Otherworlds part and you find yourself standing on the shore of an enchanted island. Priestesses greet you with yellow blossoms and a violet cloak with silver circles. You feel well cared for as they lead you to meet the Goddess Arianrhod. You notice she is standing beside the silver circle that brought you to the Otherworld. Thirteen large white owls perch close by in pale birch trees. They observe you carefully.

Arianrhod turns and smiles at you, pleased that you have found your way to her enchanted island. She asks if you are ready to understand your place in the ancient Wheel of Life. Check with your body to see if you are ready for the answer, if so, receive the worlds she offers you. Feel the gentle and loving pulses that support you and offer life to you always. For a moment, you might feel as though you are spinning with the stars in the vast universe.

Notice that above your head Silver Threads are beginning to form a larger Silver Circle. Arianrhod is teaching you how to become a Silver Artist and design with the patterns of the Great Goddess. As you acknowledge its presence, the Circle begins to glow brightly. You have the sense that the Light from this ancient Wheel informs your life, as well as your dreams and visions.

All at once the Silver Wheel shoots across the sky and joins an even greater Silver Circle that radiates in the form of a large Silver Star. Notice that the Silver Star has cast a ray of Light in your direction, and it is inviting you to walk across the nighttime sky. You reach up and take the thread of starlight in your fingertips. The Silver Thread has a pulse, as though it is the umbilicus of your soul. Take a few deep breaths and feel your connection to the universe. Suddenly you are flying through time, space and dimension.

As you come close to the enormous Silver Star you can see reflected in the light of the star the faces of your loving ancestors who smile encouragingly to you. You might also hear music and listen to the way in which Arianrhod hums life into existence. Several babies have gathered by the Silver Star waiting for an opportunity to be reborn. As you look closely, you notice that the Silver Star has a spinning vortex at its center. Although you wish to touch the center, you refrain.

"Not yet," she says. "All things return to the Great Mother through there. Instead, let's see the optimal design of your life."

Arianrhod strums her fingers across the Silver Star, and an image forms of you in the near future. You have a sense of health, accomplishment and personal well-being. In this moment, you feel in right relationship to all things.

"This is yours," she says, handing you a gift. "Treat it with utmost respect."

Now start to become aware of the gift's shape, sound, colour and texture.

"Each person is unique," she tells you. "Each person has a specific life purpose and mission. For some, great acts have been selected, others choose to tend a child or help things grow. Every detail matters, and the Earth would be bereft without you."

Sensing your place in the world and in your community, you share with the Goddess why you have come to Earth and why your life is a blessing. The Goddess listens quietly until you have finished.

"Now teach others how to find their Silver Thread," she says, fading into the air. "So they will always be able to find their way to me."

As you soar through the air, you celebrate the miracle of your birth and every detail of your design. A large white owl accompanies you. The bird carefully lands by a Silver Birch, and you notice that a wand has been carved with your name on it. Clutching the wand in its three talons, the owl offers the wand to you.

"It's your magic," says the owl. "Never forget."

The owl acts as a guide taking you back to the place and time where your journey began. He spirals down carefully making sure that all of your insights and gifts from the Otherworld come with you.

When you see your physical form, take a moment to sense the magical transformations that have taken place within your essence. Your spirit self slips back into your physical form bringing the gifts and messages from Arianrhod and the Otherworld with it. Stretch and integrate the ways in which your journey has informed your life. Take three deep breaths. When you are ready, open your eyes to a new moment.

Blessings From Trees
Song of the Birch

I touch your white bark

And teeter at the edge

As if grasping for something

I almost remember, a faint

Rustling of leaves.

I lean forward to embrace

Rough bark but with some twist of fate

I am falling…

It isn't terrifying

Just moving through space

Like a white moth caught in the breeze.

A gateway to the east has opened.

As I look into the rising sun, I see them --

The ancient gods and goddesses --

Blinking with astonishment.

Birch Ogham

BLODEUWEDD

(pronounced "Blod-u-with")

Blodeuwedd In Welsh Mythology
Woman of Flowers

Blodeuwedd is not born into the world in the usual way. Before she was a woman, she was a flower or a deva of the wild places that help flowers grow. Since Arianrhod had laid a *geis* upon Lleu that he would never marry a human woman, two magicians gathered with the intention of creating a woman from flowers for the youth. Although Math fab Mathonwy and Gilfaethwy are generally given credit for the conjuring of Blodeuwedd, it may be that Arianrhod was also secretly part of the making of Blodeuwedd, whose name means flower-face.

Not being of the human race, Blodeuwedd was not happy with the destiny she was bound to, nor was she versed in human morals. In the *Mabinogion,* she becomes lusty, is accused of adultery and attempted murder, and then is turned into an owl by her creators. Arianrhod, having already been tricked by several men, might have been more lenient as Blodeuwedd's creator. The English writer Robert Graves is more forgiving of Blodeuwedd's behavior than most, arguing that because she is an ancient Goddess she therefore operates out of the traditions of another age. Perhaps our generation will understand her.

The Myth of Lleu Llaw Gyffes

Bright One of the Skillful Hands

Lleu Llaw Gyffes is a Welsh God or Hero, and he may be related to the Irish divinity Lugh. Lleu was the premature son of Arianrhod and her poet-brother Gwydion, who kept the boy in a magical chest until he was fully formed. In Wales, the mother

traditionally names the children. However, Arianrhod refused to name the boy, feeling deceived by Gwydion after he had asked for her assistance. Eventually Gwydion tricked her once again, and as a result she named the child Lleu Llaw Gyffes, which means "bright one of the skillful hands."

According to Welsh tradition, a mother also is meant to give her son weapons, which Arianrhod initially refused to do too. Once again, she was tricked and Lleu became a warrior. Arianrhod's curse on Lleu Llaw Gyffes was that her son would never wed a human woman. Instead, a woman was formed out of flowers for him, which is where this tale begins.

Blodeuwedd's Missing Story
Love in the Meadow

When the rains came in the springtime, and the sun warmed the oak forest, a deva of the meadow called Blu felt the desire to help the yellow broom and primrose flowers blossom. She raised herself up during the twilight hours, when the starlight sings and the roots of the plants touch like lovers. All the nature spirits knew each other well in the woods, and made space for one another. Many had a particular season they loved best. The oaks communicated with the nature spirits in those days. They all enjoyed the open field in early summer, when the meadowsweet bloomed and the deer came to rest at night.

The nature spirits knew about hunters and how the animals hid from them. The spirits also feared the hunters, and they pulled the life force from flowers before the tender petals were bruised by boots of men or the hooves of horses. Still, they were curious about the human world. Men brought chaos and laughter into an otherwise peaceful existence.

One afternoon close to dusk, the shadowy magician and king, Math fab Mathonwy, and his nephew, Gwydion, came into the meadow and began picking blossoms from the broom bushes, primroses, cockles and meadowsweet flowers. They were also gathering young oak leaves. The pair chanted as the sun sank behind the tall oaks, and an eerie mist began to fill the valley. The songbirds distrusted the men's words and grew silent. Soon white-faced owls began to land on the tallest trees out of curiosity.

As the light of the full moon began to weave its way between the branches, Blu could also see the owls gathering. The spirits of the flowers were drawn to the men's enchantment as well as the birds. Blu, the deva who had been singled out by the magicians to come forth, was the same deva who helped the primroses, meadowsweet and other wildflowers grow. She enjoyed the feeling of bees and butterflies on the stalks of flowers. She also liked the way the roots interwove and the pulse of life they would bring from the nearby spring.

The Goddess Arianrhod stood beneath the oak and hazel trees watching the two magicians weaving spells. Perhaps creation was listening to them too, but when the Goddess spoke a silver ray from the moon touched some fallen oak leaves. With the guidance of the Goddess, the deva found herself being drawn to the shape the magicians were creating.

Arianrhod looked compassionately at the lovely deva for a moment and said, "Dear sweet flower spirit, there are times when the world of men will call upon you, as they have called me in the past. Forgive me, for though I already know they will love your beauty, I know too that in their ignorance they will also attempt to control you and eventually to crush you. Even so, I ask your permission to give you woman-like form."

Blu nodded in agreement, somewhat excited at the prospect of having a body. The deva had never felt the sensation of being separate from the forest. There had simply been the soil, the rain, the sun, the moon and the changing seasons. Curious about the being she might become, Blu rose up as a misty figure and looked at the Goddess.

"Speak child," said Arianrhod.

As the Goddess waved her hand, the deva felt herself becoming separate from the flowers and taking on a new structure that divided itself out from the others who grew in the woods. The nature spirits looked on with great curiosity and then drew back as the newly formed flower-faced Goddess stood with ghostly feet in the meadow.

"I have… a voice," she said hesitantly.

"Your name is now Blodeuwedd and you will be very beautiful, and eventually wise," noted Arianrhod. "If you choose to undertake this mission."

"What would you have me do, Goddess?" the flower-faced one asked, bowing to Arianrhod.

"Live in the world of men," Arianrhod answered.

After exploring her arms and legs, Blodeuwedd began to dance under the shadows of the oak and hazel trees. She smiled at Arianrhod, feeling happy with her new body.

"Stand in the place where the magicians weave their magic, so the two believe it is they who have made you. I will come too."

Arianrhod stepped out of the shadows of the oaks and strode toward the meadow where Gwydion and Math flicked their wands toward the oak leaves and wildflowers. Beside Arianrhod walked Blodeuwedd.

"Once again I have responded to your call," said Arianrhod to her brother Gwydion, who she knew was attempting to make a wife for their son. He turned and looked at her with surprise.

Glowering back at her brother, she continued. "I see you're still playing with the black magic of Uncle Math, and you have forgotten the life-affirming ways of the Goddess. No good will come of this."

She did not look at Math, who was stepping back toward the wood's shadows where even the light of the moon would be hidden. "I told you our son Lleu would not have a wife born of a woman," Arianrhod told Gwydion.

She then turned and looked sharply at Math fab Mathonwy, who was still retreating in the direction of the dark woods. "So Uncle, are you at war with some poor soul or has your *geis* been lifted?" she asked. "I see you *can* stand on the ground without a virgin foot-holder's assistance after all." Scowling at him, she added, "I'm glad you're not wasting the time of another Goddess."

"Math can stand now that he has married Goewin and redeemed our brother's error," said Gwydion.

"Not for long, I suspect," said Arianrhod. She frowned at the King, and sent a silencing spell his way.

Mathonwy looked at her unable to speak, wondering if he should flee or fight. She laughed as his tangled web of thoughts registered in her mind.

"You have nothing to fear from me, Math fab Mathonwy," Arianrhod mocked. "You need only fear what walks in the shadows of your own making. You will eventually be able to speak and walk again once I have left this valley."

Both men studied Blodeuwedd, who was radiantly beautiful in her nakedness. Her young skin was fair and unblemished, like that of a ripe fruit ready to be plucked. As the light of the moon wrapped around her like a wreath, it seemed as though a sweet woodland perfume came from the mist around her. When Blodeuwedd turned to look at the men, her light-green eyes and the perfect symmetry of her face made them gasp.

"All men will want Blodeuwedd," observed Arianrhod. "Yet she was created to be the lover and wife of Lleu, my son."

Turning to Blodeuwedd, Arianrhod said, "Lleu will love you for a while."

Gwydion strode toward his sister beaming. "You have acknowledged our son at last!" he exclaimed.

Arianrhod grew in height and strength, standing her ground against the brother she loved. "The Goddess renews herself in many ways," she told him firmly. "I accept Lleu as *Her* child. There is a place in this world for all things born of the Goddess."

"I respect you, Great Goddess," said Gwydion.

In this moment, when the stars wove light into his curls and sea-green eyes, she almost forgot his betrayal and how he had exposed her to Math's evil magic. Gwydion was attractive, and the moon seemed to make the illusion of his beauty even stronger. Even though he looked at her longingly, she would not return his gaze.

Blodeuwedd was enjoying her new body, and she skipped happily through the moonlit meadow sprinkled with wildflowers. Occasionally she would put her foot on a sharp stone and cry out. Then she would chase an owl, or lick the pollen off a flower.

"Make sure she is a vegetarian," instructed Arianrhod. "Remember to tell Lleu. And she must learn something of the ways of the world."

Math was fixated on the young girl.

"She is not for you," stated Arianrhod haughtily. "If you place your grubby hands on her, she will turn into an owl and be lost to all men."

Math looked angrily at Arianrhod, and he opened his mouth to speak, but his words blew out to sea just before another blast of wind knocked him off his feet.

"Best call your virgin foot-holder Mathonwy, oh great King of Gwynnedd, your *geis* is catching up with you, and if I do not fight you, soon you will grow weak!" Arianrhod taunted, looking down on Math. "The world is a tricky place without someone to hold you."

Arianrhod turned and walked gracefully back toward the other side of the oak forest, but stopped just before entering the shadows. She called out to the flower-faced girl, "Blodeuwedd… I created you so that you may turn my son Lleu into a hero. That is your purpose. Because you know nothing of the ways of the human world, I lay this *geis* upon you. If you ever betray Lleu, you will turn into an owl, and will live henceforth with me learning the ways of the wise Goddess. Your nighttime cry of 'whoooo' will remind us that it is the Goddess *who* we must serve."

Blodeuwedd nodded, though just half-understanding Arianrhod's words. Math sat helplessly in the dark meadow unable to stand.

Gwydion approached the flower-faced Goddess carefully and placed his violet cape across her delicate shoulders. She tried to knock the cloak away, but Gwydion said gently, "Blodeuwedd, you must learn that a woman covers herself in clothes the way a rose bush covers herself in thorns and blossoms. Without clothes, you will be picked before your time and will live prematurely with my sister."

Under the light of the full moon, Math sat in the tall grasses looking at them with disgust, beheading nearby dandelions. Blodeuwedd looked at Math and smiled. Then she picked a mature dandelion plump with seeds ready to fly and, giggling, blew them in Math's direction.

"Come with me and I will take you to Lleu," said Gwydion. "It's time you meet your destiny."

Blodeuwedd's startling light-green eyes grew wide with alarm.

"I will not harm you," Gwydion assured her. "I might be one of the only men on Earth wise enough to listen to my sister Arianrhod, for her magic is stronger than most."

Blodeuwedd blushed as Gwydion helped her onto his stallion in the darkness. She liked the way his rough hands felt on her skin, and also the way the smooth horse hair moved against her thighs. She smiled at Gwydion, and he looked away, glad she was somewhat hidden by the shadows of night.

"I will ask your wife Goewin to come with a chariot to collect you in the morning," Gwydion yelled to Math, who sat in the grass cursing the spot he was still magically bound to in the meadow. As Gwydion turned back toward Blodeuwedd, the moonlight was shining on her. He noticed the cape had slipped exposing her young left breast, which he wished he could suckle. He imagined her milk would taste like ambrosia.

"Who?" asked Blodeuwedd.

The word startled Gwydion, who realized that this could be her only available word unless he controlled his lower nature.

"I will take you directly to Lleu," he told her, taking hold of the horse's reins. Gwydion then walked briskly toward his son's cottage and prayed the moonlight would show him the way. He soon noticed that a sliver of light ran through the dark forest. Gwydion followed the strand, making sure he placed each footstep on the thread, for it showed the way the Goddess wished him to walk.

Gwydion did not stray from his task, but walked all night under the protective cloak of darkness. This was despite the several times that Blodeuwedd brushed her fine fingers against his, and he felt excitement in his manhood.

It is a good thing Arianrhod put a geis *on you,* he thought. *For otherwise, you would be deflowered before the sun has time to rise.*

Gwydion could see Lleu's home in the distance, just as the first rays of dawn presented the damp tall grasses sparkling with silver spider webs. The youth heard his father's voice calling for him, and he came bounding out of the house with his sword strapped to his back.

Lleu hugged Gwydion, but when he saw Blodeuwedd he blushed from head to toe. Being a young man, he was still new to the arts of love.

"This is your wife, Blodeuwedd," announced Gwydion, stepping over to his horse and allowing the cape to fall away from Blodeuwedd's naked form.

Blodeuwedd smiled and slid off the stallion. Gwydion noticed that there was not a mark of sweat on the beast, as if the woman had never been there.

Blodeuwedd walked to Lleu and asked, "Who are you?"

"I am Lleu," he said simply.

"My lover and husband?" inquired Blodeuwedd.

Lleu looked desperately at his father for help.

"Yes," answered Gwydion for his son, "he is your husband. I will call the Druid for your hand-fasting ceremony."

But Blodeuwedd was too quick to wait for the Druid. She placed her long shapely fingers on Lleu's flushed cheeks and breathed through his lips in the way only a flower deva can. That sort of breath sends the warmth of healing all through your body. When Blodeuwedd kissed Lleu in the open air, all he could see was blue lightning. Lleu desired her in a way that he had never longed for another.

By the time the Druid arrived, the door to Lleu's house was locked. No one saw the pair for several weeks and then just long enough to tie the hand-fasting cords around their clasped hands as a sign of their union. Then, for many years after they had been married, Lleu and Blodeuwedd were rarely seen.

After seven years, Lleu was called away into battle. He did not care to leave Blodeuwedd, yet the time had come to serve his king and country. For several days after Lleu's departure, Blodeuwedd wept for her lost love. Eventually, she busied herself rooting flower bulbs, knowing that autumn was the time to plant for spring. The cold winds came and snow covered her garden. But, unlike the devas of the fields, Blodeuwedd could not sleep through winter, for she was no longer part of that world. Throughout wintertime, she looked out the window pining for her husband.

In springtime, the thousands of flowers that she had planted burst forth, sending perfume across the land. It was a warm day in May when Gronw Pebr, the Lord of Penllyn, rode by on his bay stallion and saw Blodeuwedd bathing in a stream by the flowers. He dismounted and entered the water. She called out to Lleu, to Gwydion, and to Arianrhod, but the Lord of Penllyn was strong and he took her that day.

At first Blodeuwedd was afraid of Gronw. Yet soon she realized that although he had overpowered her, he was also skilled in the art of love. Blodeuwedd relaxed into his body and began to enjoy herself. His curly dark hair fascinated her, as did his rough hands and dark skin. As the sun began to set and the sky filled with pink and coral clouds, her body shook and Blodeuwedd experienced her first orgasm. Her husband was a novice and this was beyond what she had known with Lleu. It seemed as though Gronw Pebr was a great stag, and she was the May Queen of the land. As they made love, it was as if the flowers in the land shared their colours and scents with all of creation.

Night dropped a dark cover over the countryside, and Blodeuwedd shivered. She felt the moonlight touching her skin and remembered what Arianrhod had told her. Gronw Pebr left her beside the stream and mounted his horse without uttering a word. Blodeuwedd started to hurry to her cottage, and it seemed as though her feet curled beneath her making it hard to run. As she looked down, Blodeuwedd could see that her feet were becoming talons.

"What is your name?" cried out the Lord of Penllyn to her fleeing shadow. While waiting for an answer, he did not know she was becoming an owl. Soon Blodeuwedd circled above him, and all she could utter was "Whoooo."

Blodeuwedd, in the form of an owl, flew straight to Arianrhod, who was waiting for her in the oak forest. The Goddess observed the green-eyed owl, and nearly walked away. Blodeuwedd flew around her crying out, "Whooooo!" as only an owl can.

"Exactly," said Arianrhod. "Who did this to you?"

The owl landed on Arianrhod's cloaked shoulder and pressed her face into the hair of the Goddess. Arianrhod softened. "I might regret this," she muttered. With the flick of her hand, she turned Blodeuwedd back into a woman.

"That was a warning," cautioned Arianrhod. "I sense that Gronw Pebr overpowered you, and so I do not consider this a betrayal of Lleu. But if you choose to be with Gronw again, I will not change you back to your maiden form. You are my son's wife and were made for that purpose, and that purpose alone."

Blodeuwedd cried and wrapped her naked form around the Goddess, thanking her.

"You will stay with me until Lleu returns from battle," Arianrhod told her. "He will return soon."

Blodeuwedd blinked back her tears. "I believe I prefer life as a flower deva. It is much simpler. I ache so much now I fear my heart might break."

"Humans suffer," acknowledged Arianrhod. "Until you learn to keep your commitments to others and are free of your desires, you too will suffer."

"I'm sorry," said Blodeuwedd.

Arianrhod turned and touched the girl's right cheek with a gentle hand. Then she pulled the naked girl under her cloak for warmth and protection.

"Soon it will be time to learn to weave the starlight," noted Arianrhod. "But first you must choose above all things to work with life and not against it. If I see your future clearly, you will struggle with pleasure, passion and desire for some time to come. Often it is best to understand our mission in life and flow with it. But how can a flower refuse what feels good to her?" Arianrhod sighed.

Several months later, Lleu returned to find his home empty and his wife gone. He raced through the rooms of his home looking for his beautiful wife and calling her name, but there was no reply.

Lleu was fair in complexion, and his body was beginning to turn from that of a boy into that of a man. His shoulders had broadened, and though still young, he wore the scars of battle now.

He thought that perhaps his father Gwydion would know what had happened to Blodeuwedd. Lleu took off on his faithful golden chestnut horse, Melyngan Mangre.

As Lleu rode up to his father's house looking frantic, Gwydion was mounting his horse. He already knew what was wrong through his magic.

"When you need to find your wife, ask her mother," advised Gwydion. "A mother and child are never far apart. Let's ride to see Arianrhod in Caer Sidi."

Still seated upon his golden horse, Lleu followed in the wake of his father.

"Blodeuwedd is *not* her child," shouted Lleu, somewhat confused as Gwydion's white horse broke into a trot.

"She created Blodeuwedd from the flowers of the field and the oak leaves of the forest," Gwydion yelled back, spurring his horse into a full run. "She is your mother's gift to you."

"My wife feels like a woman to me," hollered Lleu, watching his father gallop toward the west as the sun was setting over the snowcapped hills.

Soon Lleu caught up with his father and began to overtake him. Then he fell back and followed, as it was Gwydion who knew the shallow paths that led across the sea to Caer Sidi.

They entered the grounds around his mother's sanctuary under the moonlight. Arianrhod was awake and waiting for them, and one of her initiates led the horses away for fresh water and cut meadow grasses.

Radiant as a star, Lleu walked across the kitchen towards his wife who was happy to see him. Blodeuwedd threw her arms around Lleu, but she was soon to learn that something in him had changed. Perhaps he had seen too much of war. For night after night, even after they had returned to their own cottage, he would choose to sleep alone—often crying out as if being pursued by nightmares.

Blodeuwedd came into their parlor one evening with a cup of hot tea for Lleu. She had brewed it with some of the blue chamomile flowers that grew along the banks of the stream near the cottage.

"You don't seem the same to me," said Lleu.

"Nor you to me," answered Blodeuwedd, staring into his amber eyes.

Then he did something that she wasn't expecting. He slapped her. It was not hard, but it came as a shock, and she held her right cheek with her hands pouring healing into her reddening skin.

"Gronw Pebr, Lord of Penllyn, has been spreading the tale that he stole you from me," revealed Lleu. His piercing eyes seemed to blaze like the sun on a hot summer day as he watched for her reaction.

Blodeuwedd hesitated, not sure how to describe what had happened. Finally, the young wife cried and told her husband that she had been overpowered and that Arianrhod had rescued her. She wept and held her delicate hands gently on Lleu's curled fists.

"I was made to be your wife and for no other," said Blodeuwedd with tears streaming down her pale cheeks. Then looking down, she added, "I have no other purpose."

"I suggest you find one!" shouted Lleu, withdrawing his hands with a violence she had never seen in him before. His rage made his inner light glow with a red radiance that frightened her. Blodeuwedd stepped away from him and hid in another part of the cottage. When the first rays of morning made their way through the home's windows, she heard the pounding hooves of his horse galloping on the road. Blodeuwedd knew that Lleu had left her.

Blodeuwedd felt bereft. Autumn was approaching, and the flowers she planted had withered and faded. She felt an emptiness gnawing at her from within that she had never known as a deva of the meadow. In the forest, the roots of all plants entwined around each other, supporting and encouraging the life force of one another. Having no family in the world of men and women, Blodeuwedd began wishing to return to the ecosphere she had known before becoming a woman. Blodeuwedd felt as though she had become trapped in a home, when what she really wanted most was to feel the wind, the grasses, the leaves and the sunshine. Yet when she went outside alone, Blodeuwedd was in danger of being harmed by men.

A few weeks went by and, as winter approached, Blodeuwedd became increasingly despondent. She cried and called out to Lleu, hoping he would hear her. No response came from her husband.

Then one crisp day, when ice had just begun to frame the windows and doors of her cottage, Gronw Pebr, Lord of Penllyn, rode by again on his bay stallion.

"Come out and be *my* queen," he called. "Lleu has abandoned you, and it is time I take Blodeuwedd as my wife."

Blodeuwedd hesitated, shivering in the shadows. But desire began to fill her belly, and she remembered the experience he had given her that day when the sunset filled the sky with every colour of the rainbow. She took a deep breath, then walked outside. Her floral dress hung in a way that revealed one slender shoulder. Gronw Pebr saw her and a smile crossed his lips.

"You must not touch me," warned Blodeuwedd. "I am under a *geis* from Arianrhod. I cannot go with you even if I wish it, for I will lose my life as Blodeuwedd."

"What if I kill Lleu and set you free?" asked Gronw.

This solution had not occurred to Blodeuwedd before. She knew that sometimes men were plucked from life early in battle and that women remarried.

"He cannot be killed," said Blodeuwedd.

"All men can be killed," countered Gronw, dismounting from his horse. She did not run but observed his large and muscular body as the Lord of Penllyn prepared to visit her. Gronw reminded her of a great bull. He took the sword off from around his girth and tied it to his saddle, then tied his horse to a tree.

This man had lived outside in the elements and he smelled of sweat. It seemed to Blodeuwedd that as Gronw walked along the path to her home, the wind became icier and the flower beds whitened with thickening frost. But when Gronw stood in front of her, there was a fire in her belly, and when he breathed into her hair and along her neck, her desire for him strengthened.

"Lleu once told me that there is only one way he could ever be killed," she whispered. "It is difficult to achieve, almost impossible. But if certain conditions are met, then…"

Gronw stroked her hair, put a gentle finger to her lips, and kissed her right cheek with such tenderness and passion that she shuddered. He placed his hand firmly on her lower back, just above her buttocks. She wished for a moment that he would keep touching her, but a cramp in her feet made Blodeuwedd step back.

"Lleu can be killed in one way, but it is complex," she said then, continuing to speak softly. "How could you ever get him to stand in a way that he knows could spell his end?"

"Go on," coaxed Gronw, kissing her exposed shoulder, and running his fingers inside her dress toward her breasts.

Blodeuwedd shuddered again, for a moment feeling as if she were a flower in the field. In her mind, it became spring, and the bees were buzzing around her, smelling her sweet scent, and collecting her pollen. It did not matter to the meadow how many bees visited her. She wondered why it was so important in the human world. Gronw pulled her dress down suddenly, exposing her breasts and perfect fair body. She shivered once again but let him smell her. Certainly there was a perfume arising from within her that he could not resist.

Then Blodeuwedd wondered if Arianrhod was watching them with her inner eye. She pulled her dress back up, but did not step away from the Lord of Penllyn.

"We must wait…" she managed.

"I will think of something and wait for the right moment," murmured Gronw. "I will be patient."

Despite his words, Blodeuwedd's powers overwhelmed him. Gronw grabbed her roughly and began to fondle her as she struggled. Again she experienced an orgasm.

"Tell me how Lleu can be erased, so we can be together every night. Would you like that?" asked Gronw of Blodeuwedd, who was imagining herself in the springtime meadow once again. This time a stag was visiting.

Blodeuwedd sighed. "This is the rest of what Lleu told me. He can only be killed when he has a foot in one world and his other foot in another world, and then only with a spear forged over a year."

Gronw smiled, but his time his eyes were dark. He pulled Blodeuwedd close to him.

"The *geis*," she whispered. "Arianrhod would not forgive us this time."

Gronw hesitated, then released her. He observed her body, smelled her and then he threw Blodeuwedd to the ground and took her once again.

When she heard the stallion's hooves clatter away, Blodeuwedd opened her eyes. She felt tangled and bruised. While standing up, she felt her feet turning into talons. In the darkness, Blodeuwedd whispered to the shadows that watched her, "Please, please, set me free."

Her feet twisted into talons, her eyes grew round and wide. Wings sprouted from her back, warm tawny feathers covered her. Blodeuwedd liked the idea that her form was no longer desirable because the world of men confused her. There seemed to be a list of unspoken rules that no one had told her, yet a fierce demand that she obey them all. For a while she blinked, wondering what would become of her. Was she destined to live as a shadow in the forest? Then once more she flew to Arianrhod to beg to be released from the *geis*.

Arianrhod was waiting for the owl amongst a grove of oaks in the forest, and she blew silver Light onto Blodeuwedd and turned her back into a woman, even before the owl-maiden requested it.

"I believe you like Gronw," said the Goddess. "He brings you pleasure."

"He does not," denied Blodeuwedd, who was stretching the cramps out of her toes. "He simply takes what he wants."

"What is it that you wish?" asked Arianrhod.

"I wish to be set free from all men so I can learn to weave the sounds the stars make when unfurling life on Earth," pleaded Blodeuwedd. "Please free me."

Arianrhod looked deeply into Blodeuwedd's spring-green eyes, reading her future. "My son is not yet through with the teachings you will bring him, for it is up to you to turn him into a hero."

Tears ran quietly down Blodeuwedd's cheeks, but Arianrhod turned away.

It was spring, and the flowers were opening to feel the full warmth of the sun and send their perfume across the greening hills. Lleu once again returned and collected Blodeuwedd from Caer Sidi.

"Do not leave her alone for an instant," warned Arianrhod. "For Gronw intends to kill you and take your bride as his wife."

"All of this drama over a magical flower," said Lleu. "Aren't there enough daisies in the meadow for everyone?"

"You need to honor what you have been given, or you could lose her."

"Then it is time for her to give me a child," said Lleu. "If there is enough woman in her to do that natural human task."

"Let it be so," said Arianrhod.

Blodeuwedd overheard their conversation and wished to run away, but realized that she had as much freedom to flee as the oaks in the forest during a fire. She thought of the way the pinecones would open and spew their seeds after the wildfires raged. It was the way they had of continuing life. Blodeuwedd wished again that life could be simple and that she could just help the flowers grow.

"Raising children is not so different," said Arianrhod, intuiting Blodeuwedd's thoughts.

Blodeuwedd rode meekly with Lleu back to their cottage. He offered his hand to help her dismount but she chose to slide off her mare in her own way.

The house seemed empty. Lleu threw open the shutters so light could stream in through the windows and they could feel the fresh spring air.

"I wish you knew how to keep a house," he grumbled, looking around at the cobwebs and spiders that had gathered. Blodeuwedd liked spiders, so she wasn't sure what displeased him.

I wish there were no houses, but only meadows, thought Blodeuwedd, but she dared not utter the words. For her, houses were prisons.

That night Lleu came into Blodeuwedd's bed and placed his hand on her belly. "I want children," he said.

Blodeuwedd did not respond, nor did she try to stop him from entering her. He finished quickly and soon fell asleep.

For seven nights he visited Blodeuwedd in the same way, but she felt little pleasure. For seven nights she despondently allowed him in. During the daylight hours, he stayed close to Melyngan Mangre, his golden chestnut horse, watching his wife as she tended her flowers along the stream.

After the week was over, he took Blodeuwedd back to Arianrhod and said, "I want no wife or children." And then he rode away.

Arianrhod placed a violet healing cape over Blodeuwedd, who shook from cold and an inner rage that comes from too much emptiness.

Gronw Pebr, the Lord of Penllyn, watched Lleu for weeks, waiting for the right moment to kill him. One morning Gronw spied Lleu sleeping near a stream. Grown waited nearby with a spear he had purchased from a Druid who had forged it for over a year. It had cost him a purse of gold, but Gronw desired it above all things. That is, all things except for Blodeuwedd, who he intended to win and keep.

The sun was just beginning to rise. As Lleu opened his eyes and stretched, the time was between night and day, and so the men stood between two worlds.

Lleu took his cup down to the river to a place between two thorn trees, where it is said two worlds meet. He placed his left foot into the cold water while leaving his right foot on the shore. Gronw took aim and hurled the spear at Lleu's heart with a mighty force. The spear struck him, and there was a loud crack of thunder and a flash of light so bright that it knocked Gronw backwards. Lleu grabbed the spear, which had entered the left side of his groin, and pulled it out. As the weapon fell to the ground, wings sprouted from Lleu's spine and he transformed into a golden eagle. He swooped over Gronw, who lay weaponless on the ground, and with razor-sharp talons cut his face. Gronw yelled out in pain and swung his sword at the eagle, who screeched as it flew toward the rising sun.

Lleu flew to his father Gwydion, who tended his wounds and with the help of Arianrhod transformed their son back into a man. The transfiguration changed him. Lleu's skin became increasingly radiant, his hands were hot to the touch, and he became fierce, for the eagle still lived on within him.

Blodeuwedd was suddenly startled by a vision that Lleu had been injured, but she slipped away to find Gronw Pebr. Although resisting it, the flower-maiden was drawn to Gronw in a way she didn't understand. It was as if the shadows of night had been whispering to Blodeuwedd, teasing and taunting her. She missed Gronw's attention and his rough hands that knew exactly what to do. She rode her mare to the meadow that loved her, calling out Gronw Pebr's name and weeping.

As Blodeuwedd continued on into the forest looking for Gronw, Arianrhod appeared beside her.

"You do remember that if you betray my son, you will become an owl for eternity?" she asked.

"Not if he dies first," Blodeuwedd hissed. "Then I am free. Gronw told me so."

Arianrhod was silent for a moment, as if searching for a solution. "Death does not free you from a *geis*," she pronounced at last.

Blodeuwedd cried out with such pain that it startled the deer, which then ran deeper into the forest. "Please free me from this!" she begged Arianrhod.

"When you were only a deva of a meadow, you agreed to be Lleu's wife," the Goddess reminded her.

"I had no idea what that would mean!" wailed Blodeuwedd. "I helped flowers grow. Men confuse me. Besides Gronw has killed my husband."

"Lleu cannot be killed," refuted Arianrhod. "He is the eternal sun, and although the sun sleeps at night, he returns in the morning. The flowers also sleep in winter and are raised up again in the spring."

"And are burned by the sun in the summer!" exclaimed Blodeu-wedd. "You have cursed me beyond what any woman could bear."

"My son lives and so does the life that grows within your womb," said Arianrhod. "Would you forsake her also?"

Blodeuwedd reached down and stroked her slightly distended belly.

"Soon you will give birth to a daughter of the Goddess. Lovers come and go, but we are always bound to our children," stated the wise Arianrhod. "Even if their conception seems like a trick of fate."

Hearing hoof steps, Blodeuwedd looked to her right and saw Gronw Pebr, Lord of Penllyn, riding toward her surrounded by an army of 50 men.

Suddenly Lleu stepped out from behind a boulder. The Light that shone from his body made Gronw's bay stallion rear, and the Lord of Penllyn was thrown. Many of his men's horses also reared, tossing off their riders and running away into the protection of the oaks.

"I believe you have come for my wife who is carrying my child," said Lleu.

Gronw Pebr looked surprised by this apparition of Light. "You... you died by my spear," he stammered.

"I did not die," refuted Lleu. "But am made whole by the Light that never fails."

"Are you sure it is your child she carries?" asked Gronw with a laugh.

"Children come from the Goddess, and it is our job to protect them. Or have you forgotten whose side you belong to, dark Lord?" shouted Lleu, holding up his spear. "Since you wounded me, it is now my time to deliver a blow to you."

The Lord of Penllyn looked to his men for protection, but they had backed away from the radiance of Lleu. Gronw unsheathed his sword and prepared to fight, but Arianrhod stepped between them.

"I created Blodeuwedd and I can uncreate her," declared the Goddess. "She is an illusion and not worth the pain and suffering you are preparing to put yourselves through. Blodeuwedd is a flower deva of the fields, nothing more and nothing less."

Gronw cried out to his men once again, but they knew he had raped the girl. They did not come to his aid. Lleu held his spear aloft.

"If I can stand with a stone between us, instead of a Mother Goddess, then I will receive the blow," Gronw proposed.

Arianrhod nodded and Gronw stepped out of sight behind a boulder. Lleu took aim carefully. The spear was hurled with the skill of a God and hero. It went through the boulder, and the displaced part of the stone struck Gronw Pebr, the Lord of Penllyn, in the heart, killing him instantly.

Blodeuwedd saw Gronw lying in a pool of blood and ran towards him crying. "Do not die, Lord of Penllyn," she sobbed. "I love you!" But before she could reach his body, her feet curled. She flew up in her owl form into an oak tree above the two men and cried out, "Whoo-whoo."

Lleu looked at the bird and then back at his mother.

"I cannot change her back again," Arianrhod told him. "She will be a shadow of the night now, reminding us that murder only leads us deeper into the shadows."

"I murdered him, Mother," said Lleu. "And with the weapon you gave me. Lord Penllyn took an interest in her when I did not, and perhaps she is carrying my daughter."

"She carries the daughter of the Goddess," Arianrhod corrected. "For she is not human-born."

The owl landed on Lleu's shoulder and blinked at him with startling light-green eyes.

"Do not tell a soul about this," advised Arianrhod. "For it is best that the flower-faced maiden remains hidden from desiring eyes."

Then Arianrhod began to whisper words that were known when the world was created, and she made time go back to the moment Lleu announced that he no longer desired a wife or child.

"Change your words and your desire," Arianrhod told him. "And if it humors the Great Goddess, she may change your destiny."

As Arianrhod sang, a mist was woven between the trees that awakened and began to sway. The trees were to decide if Blodeuwedd's seed could continue to grow. Arianrhod took her staff and hit the ground so hard that the trees shook. The cones of the pine trees responded by spilling their seeds onto the soft bed of needles below their old trunks. Arianrhod nodded to them and sang the ancient song once again. The owl screeched once, then Blodeuwedd took the form of a human girl again. This time, there was a young girl by her side.

Lleu went to them, knelt down and wept. "Please forgive me for my ignorance. I forgot to honor life. I see my error."

Blodeuwedd was beginning to fade back into the mist. She called out to her daughter, who turned, walked to Blodeuwedd's side, and took her hand.

Arianrhod looked kindly at Blodeuwedd and asked, "Would you choose to live amongst the women of Tir Na Ban? The Sidhe live between earth and water, and they are much more akin to the devas from which you arose. You are at liberty to do as you wish."

"Yes," answered Blodeuwedd. "I wish to be free. I wish for my daughter's freedom also."

Arianrhod gazed at the child, who looked back at her with innocent watery blue eyes. "Ah, one of the Ladies of the Lake," she said.

Turning to Lleu, Arianrhod asked, "What is your wish?"

"That Blodeuwedd and all women be free to choose the destiny of their own making," Lleu answered.

For a moment, the sun was darkened by the clouds and it rained softly.

Arianrhod placed her staff in the ground and proclaimed, "By enabling my son to become a hero, Blodeuwedd has earned her right to choose. She and her child have earned their right to do as they will."

Blodeuwedd then took her daughter's hand and walked toward the spring that had emerged from the stones bordering the hill that lay above them. Lleu watched as a doorway opened and a wave took them. It was one of the portals of the Sidhe that leads to the shining land of Tir Nan Og, where life is eternal and women choose their lovers. In the blink of an eye, Lleu's wife and daughter were gone. The only sound left was the gentle wind that rustled in the branches of the old forest.

"They will live with your brother Dylan for a time," noted Arianrhod. "The people of the sea are freer in their love. He will lead them to the Land of Women."

Lleu stood, listening to the sounds around him. The trees resumed their sleep and the night grew still. Their magic was no longer needed.

"I didn't know what a great gift I had been given," lamented Lleu. "I was not ready for her until now, and she has gone."

"Her role was to turn you into a hero and she did," said Arianrhod. "When young men wish to become heroes, it is not always what they might expect."

"And she became a heroine," acknowledged Lleu.

"You have become who you are meant to be," stated Arianrhod.

"Then I will also go to my destiny and be a shining light and leader of my people," Lleu vowed, and he whistled to his stallion Melyngan Mangre. His horse galloped across the field toward him with golden mane flying.

Honoring the Goddess Blodeuwedd

Celebrating Blodeuwedd
The First Full Moon in May

Blodeuwedd is celebrated in the springtime on the first full moon in May, and during the holiday of Beltane. As a wise Goddess of beauty, sexuality and intimacy, she is called upon to bring all things into right relationship. One way to honor Blodeuwedd is to collect a bouquet of flowers, and to display it in a vase on an altar or other prominent place. The flowers associated with Blodeuwedd include Gorse, Broom (or yellow springtime flowers such as Forsythia), Meadowsweet (or Queen Anne's Lace) and Oak leaves. The Goddess loves all seasonal wildflowers.

Spring is the time of year when green leaves unfurl and all of nature begins to whisper the secrets of new life. Colourful flowers begin to open in the warming sun's rays, and with the help of Blodeu-wedd, we might become more attuned to the erotic aspect of our True Nature. Spring is the time to celebrate intimacy and partnership.

Celebrating Lleu Llaw Gyffes
Lughnasadh/Lammas

Lleu Llaw Gyffes, the Welsh aspect of the Sun God Lugh, is known for the brightness of his face, his strength, magical skills and multiple talents. Lleu is celebrated each year around August 1 on Lughnasadh or Lammas, a festival celebrating the harvest season. Lughnasadh means the games of Lugh. In myth and legend, it is said that the Goddess Taillte once resided on the magical *Temair* (Hill of Tara). In ancient Ireland, she was known as the foster-mother of the Light, who took the embodied form as the Sun God, Lugh. Lughnasadh is a time for music, feasting and story-telling. Today many people make a meal to celebrate the harvest and the feminine energy that sustains us.

Lleu Llaw Gyffes In Nature
Barley, Stallions & Bees

This proud warrior reminds us that we each have unique skills and talents. Lleu needs to claim his name, gifts and life partner in unusual ways, but he does succeed. Breads, barley wines and beers are prepared with barley, which can be used during Lughnasadh.

As a totem beast, the horse represents freedom and power. Melyngan Mangre is the name of Lleu's faithful golden chestnut stallion that can carry him over land and sea. Lleu's sacred symbol is a Honey Bee, which ensures the continuation of life.

In the Ogham tradition, the Ash tree *(Nuin)* is linked to the cosmic masculine energies of the Sun God Lugh. Lleu's father carried a wand made of Ash and was said to work magic with it.

Blodeuwedd In Nature
Owls, Rabbits, Flowers & Spiders

Blodeuwedd arises out of the Meadow Flowers, and she is accompanied by a young Owl (her sacred symbol), who is still learning the ways of this world. Both Goddess and Owl can step between the dimensions of time and space, often co-existing in the realms of the human kingdom as well as the place where the Faery-folk reside.

A Rabbit or Hare (her familiar) is also a companion to Blodeuwedd, who prefers the wild woods and meadows to a domesticated life. She is also fond of Spiders and reminds us to be careful to set them outside, where they can weave their webs in the moonlight. Blodeuwedd tends to shun social mores and live from the wildness of her own pure heart.

Blodeuwedd's Colours
Green, Coral & Rose Pink

The three colours sacred to Blodeuwedd are Green, Coral and Rose Pink. Her colour combination helps us attune to the rhythms of the Earth. In this way, like the Goddess, we can blossom into the fullness of our inherent beauty and design. This grouping of colours is called "Born to Love."

Green is the colour of plants and the Faery-folk. Goddesses who radiate Green Light work in harmony with Nature. They tend to act from the feeling side of their heart. One way to get in touch with your Green essence is to go out into a forest and simply hug a tree. Then become aware of the resulting feelings of spaciousness and freedom.

Coral is the colour of the wisdom of love. Blodeuwedd was born to love, but what we learn in our intimate relationships is that the first person we must love is ourselves. Life circumstances change, but our best friend is never farther away than our own heart. Coral helps clear issues with unrequited love and supports a move into right relationship.

Pink is the colour of unconditional love. It is the type of love that a mother has for a child. Rose pink can open us up to the possibility of spiritual sexuality, which is so needed in the world today. When people wish to be intimate with gentleness, attunement and kindness, they both can flourish.

"Born to Love"

Lleu Llaw Gyffes' Colours
Red, Yellow & Green

Lleu Llaw Gyffes' sacred colours are Red, Yellow and Green. Red is the colour of the strength that we need as spiritual warriors on the journey to discover the truth of who we are, and also to face the truth that we discover about ourselves in relationships. Yellow is related to Lleu's role as an aspect of the Sun God Lugh, and it has to do with intelligence, independence, skillfulness and joy. Green is the colour of summer meadows and trees in full blossom. Green is also the colour of a loving, open and compassionate heart.

This colour combination is used when we have a decision to make, for it helps us align with the balanced wisdom of Nature. Together, these colours reflect the decisions we are often faced with in close relationships. The combination is called:

"Decision Maker"

Meeting the Goddess Blodeuwedd

There are times when we grow tired of convention and wish to remember the wild and untamed quality of our True Nature. When you are ready to rebel, call upon Blodeuwedd to teach you the secrets of the Faery-folk. Blodeuwedd may have been confused by the laws of the human world, but she understands how flowers grow. Any time you can, throw local wild seeds into the wind, and let the sylphs carry them where they may. Follow the next practice if you want to get to know the Devic world and how you can attune to the living forces within plants.

Practice
Activating Seeds for Healing

You will need:

Soil prepared for planting

A cup filled with pure water

1 packet of organic garden seeds

A timer

Prepare a plot of soil in your garden, and set a large bowl, cup or cauldron of water beside you. Take some non-toxic seeds—such as organic lettuce, kale, carrot or sunflower seeds—and place them in the palm of your left hand. Then spit your saliva onto the seeds until they are well covered. Using your timer to track time, hold the seeds for exactly seven minutes in your closed palms. Close your eyes and feel the special life-affirming energies the seeds hold.

Done correctly, the seeds will respond to your wishes. Your saliva will dissolve the protective coating that covers the seeds, and they will begin to respond to the signals your body is sending. The seeds will then grow in a way that strengthens your health and well-being.

Now plant all the seeds. When you are done, rinse your hands in the bowl or cauldron of water, and then gently water the seeds with the water from the rinsing bowl.

In order to continue a relationship with your garden, every day call upon the devas of the fields. Early in the morning and/or late in the afternoon, take your container of water and rinse your hands, then pour the water gently over the soil of the garden. In this way, the plants can continue to respond to the needs of your body. Speak softly to the plants, and sense how each one shares a different medicine.

When it is time to harvest the plants, more often than not they will have been kissed by the devas from Tir Na Ban, and thus will help you align with your health and well-being. You might notice that they are a little sweet, and you might feel so good after eating them that you want to dance under the light of the midday sun.

Visualization
The Secrets of Flowers

Collect flowers for your altar, make sure your sacred space is set and prepare yourself to enter the Otherworlds. Close your eyes and take three deep breaths:

Imagine that it is springtime, and you are walking in a green field filled with flowers. Notice the chorus of songbirds and the vibrant world of colour of which you are a part. A rabbit runs past, and you realize that Blodeuwedd would like to take you on a journey. Ask the Goddess to guide you to a place in nature where you will discover the flower that shares the essence and design of your soul.

Blodeuwedd appears beside you in the form of a beautiful maiden with owl feathers in her hair. Thank her for being willing to help you learn about the secrets of the flowers and the magic of Nature. Follow her through a winding path that takes you past streams and along the edge of verdant forests. When you come to the appropriate place, Blodeuwedd motions for you to sit amongst the flowers.

The Flower Goddess places her left palm on your forehead. Blodeuwedd has opened up your inner vision so that you can see the mysteries of Nature that exist subtly in this world. Suddenly the sounds and colours around you become loud and distinct.

She asks you to listen to the song of your heart. Placing your hands on your heart, you listen with your inner ear. Blodeuwedd places her hands on your ears, so that your focus is drawn inwards. You might hear a tune, the song that has lived within you since birth and even before. If you don't hear it, hum any way, for your song is

93

within you. Like the songs of birds and the humming of bees, the sound is harmonizing and balancing.

Notice that there is a flower growing just in front of you. As you look carefully at the beautiful blossom, you realize that the Flower Goddess has led you to the flower that shares your song. Blodeuwedd smiles, plucks the flower and hands it to you. Look carefully at its colour and design. What colour is it and how many petals does it have? Notice if it has a scent and if so, how that makes you feel. When you are ready, receive the essence of the flower. Feel the healing Light that flows into your body and strengthens you.

Taking the flower with you, follow Blodeuwedd who has now turned into a rabbit. Return back to your body and become fully aware of this time and place. Thank Blodeuwedd for her wisdom, and know that you can call upon the essence of flowers any time you need their wisdom.

Blessing From Trees
Song of the Gorse

Forgive yourself for giving up.

Even on the evenings when the nights seem too long,

When there is no one to speak to

About suffering that seems to seep through

The cracks in your soul,

The yellow blossoms of the Gorse blow kisses.

Remember the flowers that wilt and fall,

Then bloom again, unafraid

Of the art of both living and dying.

Sniff the perfume riding lightly on breezes.

Gather up a bouquet of wild flowers

Into your tender hands,

Bring them close to your heart.

Breathe in and out –

Ask for the wisdom of the Gorse

Then, holding a yellow blossom in your hand,

Open the gateway to hope and faith,

A perfume as enduring as the sun.

Gorse Ogham

II
Finding the Goddess in British Mythology

IOUGA & ELEN

IOUGA

(pronounced "aye-ou-ga")*

---

* This is an approximation. The true pronunciation of Iouga is unknown, and may be closer to "Juga" meaning "yoke."

Iouga In British Mythology
Reconstructing the Goddess

Iouga is the reconstructed name of a Romano-British Goddess who was commemorated on a broken altar-stone in York, England. The Romano-British culture developed in Great Britain after the Romans conquered the region. This Goddess is thought to have been worshipped between 43 and 410 AD. Her name means "where two rivers meet." The Druids knew that places where rivers come together are often portals to the Otherworlds.

There are scholars who say that the true name of this Goddess was Boann or Boinn, the Irish Goddess of the River Boyne, or perhaps Boann is a Sister Goddess of Iouga's, or a daughter. Mythologically, Boann was known as the one who created the River Boyne. Others claim Iouga challenged the healing power of a well or spring and was drowned in a flood. Iouga and Boann could be the same Goddess or aspects of the women from the Otherworldly dimension of Avalon. An ancient name for the Divine is IOA. So it may be that Iouga came from the north and is connected to the holy Isle of Iona in Scotland.

Although little else is known about her, there are mystics who say that Iouga and her wisdom can still be called upon along the banks of a flowing river, and that she wishes to pass her wisdom to all her daughters. It is a myth related to her relationship with a river that follows this introduction.

Iouga's Untold Story
Whispers by the River

Once upon a time, when the Earth was full of colour and light, and she was not familiar with cold, darkness and hunger as she is now, there lived a River Deity named Iouga. She spent much time beside the springs, rivers and streams that ran through the Celtic world. Iouga had been with the Mother Goddess Danu when the great river Danube was born, and also with the Goddess Boann when the River Boyne came into existence. She especially appreciated the places where two rivers met. She loved how streams and rivers could find their way to unite and then flow in harmony as one.

Desiring to have a river of her own, Iouga spoke to the waters that flow deep inside the earth and asked if a new river could be born. The Great Mother Goddess rejoiced at her request. Soon a stream bubbled up through the ground, and a river began to flow. Iouga named the river "babble," for she knew that in truth rivers cannot have names, as they constantly spill themselves into the sea.

From that time on, Iouga enjoyed flying along the little river that had become her closest friend. Sometimes she rested lightly on the water, bathing her elegant green wings that shimmered in the light.

She and the river understood each other. This understanding was not through words; Iouga talked to the river through the feelings that bubbled within her heart. Since she was happy, the river flowed evenly around the stones and polished pebbles.

Sometimes late at night, when Iouga was ready to rest, there was a faint stirring of sadness within her. During the days, however, Iouga delighted in her awareness of the wind passing secrets through the leaves, and the birds singing their ancient songs. Iouga would spend hours each day under a cluster of three hazel trees in a grove beside her river. Their large oval leaves would comb the wind and whisper to the salmon. They urged the fish to eat the hazelnuts that had fallen in the river, for the wisdom of the Great Goddess was stored in them. Apple trees also grew close by, and Nature Spirits loved the area, for it was an easy place to slip between the worlds. For a long time, Iouga was content in this land of pastel light.

One night, Iouga began to wonder if there were other beings that lived along the edge of the broad river. She loved the river, the trees and the birds, but she longed to know another like herself. This feeling grew stronger inside her until Iouga decided to ask the Great Goddess to help her.

The very next day, the river took Iouga's message to the Great Goddess. The Goddess shared her reply with the river, who repeated it to Iouga upon returning. The message was:

"Go as I direct you. You will find the companionship you seek, and through another, you shall know thyself."

After that, the river seemed to have nothing more to say to Iouga. He just babbled and this made her feel even lonelier. Nor did the birds or trees speak to her. It was as though a strange silence had fallen upon her heart. She had also grown heavy. She no longer could fly or float lightly on the river's surface, but walked along the river dejectedly. Increasingly aware that the stones beneath her had sharp edges, she sometimes bruised her feet.

Iouga was considering making a pair of shoes for herself with some ferns, and then she heard whispers along the banks of the river. She realized that the Great Goddess was speaking to her. The Deity told her:

"Go from the river now. It is time.
You'll see a path that leads to the right.
Take it and you'll meet your future."

Sure enough, just a few yards ahead, there was a little dirt path leading to the right and away from the river. It did not look well-trodden, but Iouga trusted the voice and so she followed the path. She found herself walking through a lush meadow filled with bluebells and blue butterflies. A cloud darkened the sky, and a quick shower replenished the nearby river and watered the meadow. As the water droplets fed the freshly unfurling ferns, a double-arched rainbow appeared before Iouga. The River Deity was certain that the Great Goddess had sent the rainbow as a message that what she sought would soon be found.

The path led her into a new landscape. It was hot and dry, with red rocks and a hint of desert. She soon heard the voice from deep within again:

"When you come to the rock in the shape of a circle,
you are to climb on top.
From there, you will be taken to your destiny."

Iouga quickened her pace. Even though she could no longer fly, Iouga felt light and carefree. The path led to the top of a hillside, and there she saw an unmistakable upright blue-slate stone in the shape of a circle. Eager to find out what would happen next, she scrambled up the rock.

As soon as Iouga sat upon the top of it, the circular stone began to vibrate. It lifted off from the hillside and rose into the air like a blue bubble! Soon Iouga could see the meadow she had just walked through and then, far below, her beloved river. Mist was rising from the water, and she could make out a waterfall not far away, surrounded by a grove of hazel trees.

Then she felt the rock shift again. It tilted a little. Iouga realized how high up she was and remembered that she could no longer fly.

"I hope the stone doesn't tilt too much more," she thought. "For it is slick, and if it does tilt more, I won't be able to hold on."

The rock did continue to tilt. Iouga slid, trying with all her might to maintain her grip. Her fingers could not find any crevices to cling to on the stone. At last, she was hanging on only by her fingertips. Her body was swaying in the wind, but her wings would not hold her up. Iouga was terrified as she looked down at the river below.

"I'm too high up," she told herself, looking at the shallow riverbed. "I will be crushed on the rocks."

"Let go," whispered the Goddess. "I will hold you."

"But I'll be killed!" Iouga protested.

"I will hold you," the voice repeated.

"I'm frightened!"

"If you wish to know another like yourself, let go," said the Great Goddess.

Iouga let go, and the Goddess did not hold her up in the way she had expected. As she plummeted toward the river, all Iouga could see was the blue of the sky, then the approaching river of water and stones. Soon she hit the earth.

The next thing Iouga remembered was holding the hand of a little girl. They were walking along the banks of a pretty little river that made its way through a grove of hazel trees. Blue butterflies accompanied them as they ambled along listening to the sounds of nature.

"Listen to the river, Mama," the little girl said. "It likes to talk to you."

Iouga listened to the water flowing around the rocks. The sound reminded her of something she could not quite place, but it arose from the depths of her. She felt the tug, but wasn't sure where it would lead, and let the idea go.

The little girl stopped and began staring at the water. "Look, Mama," she said to Iouga. "Is it an angel?"

They both stared, startled by the image. There in the shallows of the river was what appeared to be an angel with open gossamer wings floating in the water. An odd, familiar feeling stirred within Iouga, but she couldn't quite place it.

How beautiful she is, thought Iouga, looking at the green form that was just beginning to decay. *How sad that such a creature should perish.*

"Maybe she is a Water Spirit," said the girl.

Iouga gazed at the body again and thought it oddly comforting to know there were other beings who lived along the river's broad banks.

Her daughter was now looking at a bush covered with blue flowers. Iouga moved toward her, still thinking about the form in the river. She noticed a path leading to the right and could see the trace of some footprints in the mud. Iouga thought about exploring the path, but felt as though she had already been that way. Yet she couldn't truly remember.

"Mama, come see!" the little girl called out merrily, as she stood at the river's edge again.

The daughter was looking at herself in the water. Iouga crouched down beside her to look at the girl's reflection.

"What is your name, child?" asked Iouga.

"Boann, silly," laughed the little girl.

Iouga looked down into the still water along the banks of the river. The dark water created a pool that formed a mirror-like reflection. At first Iouga thought she was looking at her mother, although she could hardly remember her. Nearby, the discarded body of the River Deity was being licked by the currents, and the form started to disintegrate.

As Iouga continued to peer into the water, it seemed as though she was looking into two worlds that were revealing both a past and a present moment. She wondered briefly which world was most true: the past, the present or the future.

Boann knelt down beside her mother, and they peered into the water together. As they looked down at the thin wings of the Faery that were dissolving into the play of shadow and light, Iouga could see the reflection of her daughter and herself in the water. The vision startled her, because it seemed in some way that all three were one being sharing the one great river. She took a deep breath and smiled. Iouga sensed that she had found what she had been seeking all along.

"Great Goddess, thank you," Iouga whispered, for she remembered that the many are really One.

"Look, Mama," little Boann laughed as she passed her fingertips over the surface of the water. "We look exactly the same."

Honoring the Goddess Iouga

Celebrating Iouga
Circular Stones

Iouga reminds us that we all come from the Great Goddess, and that although our forms will change with time, we are eternally held by the Mother. We can honor her by collecting circular stones for our altars.

On the Celtic Wheel of Life, Iouga and Boann can open the gateway to the west, allowing what is outdated to fall away like the skin of an eel, or the outer shell of a hazelnut. Like the wise salmon, Iouga understands the natural process of birth, death and rebirth. Having undergone her own process of transformation like a butterfly, Iouga can also open the gateway to the east, inviting in the dawn and the freshness of a new perspective on life.

Iouga's name may come from the word Iona, the name of an island off the western coast of Scotland (which was previously called *Ioua insula*). It is well known as the center of Saint Columba's monastery. In Gaelic, *Eilean Idhe* means the isle of Iona. The island has also been called *Ì nam ban bòidheach,* or the isle of beautiful women. These Gaelic names may suggest a link between Ioua, Iona, Iouga and Avalon.

Iouga In Nature
Hazel, Blue Butterfly & Salmon

Iouga continues to exist as a whisper along the banks of rivers. Each of us is aligned with special aspects of nature that help to define us. The Hazel is a tree that is well loved by Iouga, and Hazel Flower Essence can be made and used to awaken freedom and spontaneity with us. In the Celtic world, Hazel twigs and branches are worn for safety and protection. The Ogham for this tree is *Coll*, and a journey with the tree can lead you to inner wisdom.

Hazel Ogham

A totem associated with Hazel is the Wise Salmon, who can appear when it is time to acquire knowledge, especially that of a mystical nature. In folklore there is a fish known as the Salmon of Assaroe, who is meant to be as old as time.

The Blue Butterfly is another of Iouga's sacred companions, who represents the ability to shapeshift and transform. Like the butterfly, Iouga moves easily through all of her physical transformations, learning about each stage of life as she moves through the process. In Christianity, the butterfly is a symbol of the soul. In folklore there is a joyous connection between butterflies and the Faery Realm. Some say you can follow a butterfly to the Blessed Isles. Both the Butterfly and the Salmon can easily move between worlds and invite us to connect to the spiraling energies that exist invisibly around us. Iouga's favorite flowers are the Bluebells that blossom in April and May and encourage us to open our hearts and trust the process of life. Any time you are beside a stream, river or any flowing body of fresh water, remember Iouga. If you listen with the ears of your heart, you might just hear someone humming the ancient healing songs.

Iouga's Colours
Olive, Blue & Royal Blue

Iouga's three sacred colours, Olive, Blue and Royal Blue, are the colours we would find along a wide flowing river that supports many lives. A Goddess who radiates Olive light understands the wisdom of the Earth, and in her deep relaxation embodies peace and compassion. Olive is the colour of feminine power and hope for humanity. The moss and leaves of the forests remind us of an ancient time that is returning, in which we honor and accept each individual exactly as they are. Olive supports the growth of the human spirit.

Blue is a colour that helps us connect to blueprints, and our ability to create new life. It also reminds us that although forms may change, we are eternal. Blue, one of the last colours humans can see in normal awareness, invites in Divine conversation. Mystics report the perception of a blue door that opens up at death so that we may travel to meet our ancestors and loved ones. Iouga rides on a circular blue stone and learns to let go and trust destiny. Staring into the river with her daughter, she is aware that she can see her past, present and future selves simultaneously. A Goddess who radiates Blue light is aligned with her Divine blueprint and has faith in the process of life.

A person who radiates Royal Blue light has paranormal vision and the ability to see beyond the veil into the Otherworlds. The awakening of the sixth sense helps us see what was once hidden and opens us up to our true potential.

This combination of colours helps us understand that we can let go in the process of life. The colour combination is called:

"River of Destiny"

Meeting the Goddess Iouga

When we begin to wish to meet our other selves, then it is time to call Iouga. At some stage in our lives, we all encounter loneliness. Wishing to find another like herself, Iouga goes on an adventure in which she has a glimpse of her past, present and future selves. The Great Goddess asks Iouga to climb aboard a blue circular stone, and what she learns is that the circle is a symbol of our eternal nature. As in Iouga's story, we can be as solid yet still rise in the air as easily as a feather. Like the moon, we are both changeable and eternal. Stepping into the future Iouga meets her daughter, and also the remains of her outdated self. She takes it in stride as a great and eternal mystery. Iouga reminds us that we can never be alone, for we live in an alive and ever changing universe in which are all intricately connected.

Practice
Walking Meditation

To get to know all aspects of your True Nature, take time for yourself and walk to a park preferably finding a large body of water to walk beside. Use a timer if possible:

For 5 minutes, slow your walking pace so that you go half your normal speed. Listen to the flowing water and see if you can walk in harmony with its music. Take each step consciously and slowly. Speak to the water like you would a friend—remembering that water is the key to life. For 5 minutes, walk quickly and just observe how differently your body/mind feels. Then return to slow walking for another 5 minutes, or longer if you enter into harmonious dialogue with nature.

If you listen carefully, you might hear the Great Goddess in the rippling water or the whisper of the wind through the leaves. Feel deeply. If you see a butterfly, know the Goddess Iouga is accompanying you.

Visualization
The Source of the River

Imagine that you are by the banks of a flowing river. A salmon jumps up, and you realize that Iouga would like to share her wisdom with you. You notice that off to your left, there are three hazel trees. As you walk to them, one of the three trees drops nine hazelnuts. You reach down and gather them. Holding the hazelnuts in your hands, you ask Iouga to share a message with you.

Noticing a path that leads to your right, you take it. You walk up a hill that leads to an upright blue circular stone. You find a perfect crevice to sit in. The stone feels curiously soft, and then you realize that it has become as light as a feather. The stone begins to vibrate. You lift off the ground and fly on the stone along the banks of the river. Looking down, you can now understand what the river is saying. You listen to the messages the water has to share with you, and thank him for his wisdom.

Although you like to feel comfortable, journeys are not always about relaxation. Suddenly the stone turns, and you find yourself tumbling through the air toward the river. Just when you think you are going to hit the stones below, a blue door opens, and you are traveling through a tunnel. You can hear the whispers of your mothers and grandmothers who love and care for you.

Realizing that you have passed into an Otherworld, you look around at the startling display of colours, and listen to the lovely sound of bells. Three women approach you. The first woman is young and wears an olive cloak. The second woman is wrapped in a blue cloak, and she is holding a baby. The third is a wise priestess, and her royal blue robe is covered with moons and stars. The priestess hands a shimmering silver branch to you, while the others smile. You graciously accept it. Once the branch is in your hands, you sense a strong flow of life force—as though you have become a river.

"You are part of the Greater River now," says the wise priestess. "You may drink from the Source anytime you need strength and renewal."

Giving the priestess the nine hazelnuts as a gift, you step backwards and find yourself falling once again through a blue tunnel. A bubble forms around you, and you are flying along the river, that babbles and laughs, accompanied by blue butterflies. The blue bubble sets you down gently on a circular stone, and you realize that your body feels healthy and renewed.

Stretch and feel the renewed strength and wisdom that you have brought with you from the Otherworld. Thank Iouga for her gifts, and also the Salmon and Butterflies who have been your sacred companions. Also remember to thank all the mothers and grandmothers in your lineage—for we all arise out of the same river.

Blessings From Trees
Song of the Hazel

A salmon swims by the grove of hazel trees,

Nine nuts fall into the water.

The salmon circles them knowing

Once he eats the nutmeat

All men and woman will pursue him.

He thinks perhaps he can resist the hazelnuts,

Just keep swimming upstream toward home

Then decides to have just one nibble,

A taste of a secret as old as time.

In that moment he knows

Either way he will die and live again.

So why not commit to the frying pan?

Even when caught, he can leap free again and again

Slapping men and women on the brow,

Watching as they smile.

Hazel Ogham

121

ELEN

Elen In British Mythology
Lady of the Wildwood

len is generally depicted as a beautiful woman with antlers, symbolizing her sensitivity to the natural world. Elen is also known as a Lady of the Wildwood, the pulse of wild places. She is difficult to harness with myth and legend, yet her stories are still told. Elen, also known as "Elen of the Ways," is a Goddess of Sovereignty who can act as a guide during times of change. She has been worshipped since Paleolithic times and is linked to fertility and the wellbeing of the land. The archetypal story of Elen is prehistoric, depicting an ancient guide who often runs naked with reindeer along forest paths. Although she seems familiar, Elen tends to hide in the shadows until the initiate is ready. She is sometimes referred to as the Celtic Venus, or Shakti. In folklore, she follows the reindeer through ice and snow across the Boreal Forest to Britain. Usually stags grow antlers, but female reindeer also grow antlers.

In a 4th Century Romano-British tale known as "The Dream of Macsen Wledig,"* the Emperor of Rome, Magnus Maximus (who

---

* Part of the Welsh book of mythology known as *The Mabinogion.*

later is absorbed into the Welsh tradition as Mascen Wledig), is out hunting, grows tired and, during a nap, has a visionary encounter with Elen. He describes her as the most beautiful woman he has ever seen, who shines as brightly as the morning sun. Inspired by her beauty, he sends his men in search of her, but she replies that if the Emperor wants her he has to come and claim her. Mascen Wledig sets out on an adventure to Britain and asks for her hand in marriage, which she accepts. In folklore, Mascen Wledig is credited with building roads in her honor.

Mythical Elen Luyddog of the Hosts of Britain (340-388 AD) became known as Helen of Caernarfon and the mother of Constantine the Blessed. She is associated with the Roman roads in Wales. It is said that Saint Helena's pilgrimage trail once extended to Jerusalem. There are more holy wells named after Saint Helena in Britain than any other female saint. In some legends, Saint Helena of Caernarfon ordered the building of Sarn Helen, a great Roman road that runs through Wales. Some mystics say that her presence can still be felt along the great Ridgeway that connects Avebury in Wiltshire to Ivinghoe Beacon in Buckinghamshire, as well as other roads and tracks that connect Britain.

Several mystics consider Elen to be the mother of Britain's native shamanism, while others say she is Queen of Witches. Archetypally, Elen is certainly a guardian of pathways that can lead us to deeper meaning.

Elen's Secret Meeting
Secrets of the Antlered Ones

It was winter and Grandfather Holly knew his time was coming to an end. During the day he walked along the river observing the way the light reflected in each of the pools that gathered at the edge. He spoke gently to the salmon and trout, even the river snakes. Each night, when he thought we were sleeping, he would go outside. I could see him from out of my window. He would look at the moon, and then the whispers would begin. I wasn't sure where they came from but it seemed to be from the place by the river where the old yew grows. One night when the moon was full and the ground looked silver, I followed him out into the woods to observe him as he spoke to the invisible world.

An owl flew overhead and hooted which startled me, but Grandfather was not afraid. He hooted back to the owl and continued walking deeper into the forest. He seemed clear about where he was going and his purpose. Finally, Grandfather arrived to the place where the yew weaves her branches into sky and soil. He stood looking up at the night sky. I crouched by the younger oak trees, watching and waiting as Grandfather stared at the full moon. He stared for so long that I nearly left, but then I noticed an antlered stag had walked into the oak grove and was standing beside him.

"Hello old friend," said Grandfather Holly.

The stag lowered his antlers gracefully, as if bowing. I wanted to step forward because I realized how easy it would be for the stag to kill the old man. Even though he was fragile, Grandfather and the virile stag stood together, staring at the full moon.

"Has she arrived yet?" asked Grandfather.

As if on cue, a slender doe joined the two. They stood together as she walked around them, sniffing and observing them carefully.

"Elen," said Grandfather Holly. "I have loved you through all the seasons of my life."

The doe turned to look at the old man, then put her head on his chest. Under the silver rays of the full moon, the doe reared and shifted into a woman with red hair. Except for antlers and a garland of flowers, she was naked. Elen touched my grandfather's face ever so gently with her slender white hands. He gazed upon her with deep focus and affection.

"It is time to come home with me Holly," she said.

"But my wife, my family…" he protested and then pointed to me.

I stayed in my hiding place, not sure what to do. I had thought Grandfather Holly did not know I was there.

"Lily is one of us," noted Elen, calling me out from of the shadows. "Come here, child. Don't be frightened."

Grandfather nodded with gentle approval and I stepped forward to take his old gnarled hand.

"The time of his rule is done," said Elen.

"It has been a good life," said the old man.

Elen walked behind my grandfather and touched his neck. She seemed so gentle that I did not notice the shining silver of a metal blade. It was too late. Elen kissed Grandfather Holly on the cheek, and then cut his silver cord. Grandfather dropped to his knees and then fell face forward into the cold ground. I started to cry. Snow began to fall. The stag and the doe walked around Grandfather's body once and then left the forest.

Some moments passed and then I rolled his body over. It was heavy without the breath of life in it. My tears fell onto his face and for a moment I thought he smiled. I noticed a holly bush and I plucked some of the leaves and laid them on his body.

Something stirred beneath Grandfather as if the gnarled roots of the oaks were holding up their old friend. I could see there was a portal to another world, perhaps where his body would be taken back into the soil. I started to go with him but Elen was standing beside me in her womanly form.

"It is not your time to go with old man Holly," said Elen. "Mother Earth knows how to care for him. He will return in another season with a new body and a new life. But for now he must sleep in a place you cannot enter and dream the dreams of both the past and the future."

I started to weep again.

"Why do you cry, child?" asked the antlered Goddess.

"I loved him and I will miss him," I told her.

"If you love him, then sing to the Dream Time so your love for him is heard and remembered. The stars record all forms of love. It is your job now to hold up the sky.

"This is where the sun will rise," Elen said pointing to the ash trees. "When you face the east you will understand that there are many new gifts that the air wishes to carry to you."

I closed my eyes, and even though it was dark, I faced east. I thought an owl hooted, and I wondered if bats were close by. I put my arms out to the side as if to practice flying.

Elen was observing me closely. "Let go of what you don't need so the new can come."

I stood in the clearing and although it was chilly, I took off my clothes and laid them gently beneath the ash trees. I sang a song that had been sung to me by my grandmother about King Arthur who was taken to Avalon by his sister, Morgan le Fey, for healing and safekeeping until the time of his return.

Elen stood beside me, listening. Her contemplation was so deep that I started to hear and see the woods in a new way. I noticed a glimmering path that led off to the right into the forest. It looked as though it was made of ash and oak leaves, and the tracks of deer.

"Follow the tracks," whispered Elen. "This is your future, for you are still full of life."

I turned back to look at Grandfather's body, which was now covered by a mound of newly fallen snow. I knew the roots of the oaks would eventually lower him into the great river that flows west.

"He sleeps," said Elen. "But you live, so go. Perhaps you will find him in a new way."

As soon as my feet touched the path, I was flying. I looked out to see my arms, but what I saw were large owl wings. I flew south along the deer tracks until I saw the stag standing beside a large bonfire.

"Welcome," said the stag. I was drawn to him and landed beside him. As I watched, the stag twisted and transformed into a man. I observed him for a moment. His breath made steam in the air. He was muscular and attractive.

For a moment I was shy about my own nakedness. But then he reached out to take my hand, and I realized we would dance the most ancient dance of all — as God and Goddess, man and woman.

Off in the distance I could see the glimmers of dawn creating golden and pink patterns on the peaks of the mountains. And then he kissed me.

Honoring the Goddess Elen

Celebrating Elen
Opening the Way

Elen, Lady of the Wildwood, can be called upon when you are ready to take a journey either in this world or when journeying into the Otherworlds. She is a protector of the roads, and a guardian to call upon when opening gateways into new dimensions. Elen's antlers help her stay attuned to the flow of life. It was once believed that there were eight cracks during the year, known as the thin times, when it was easier to communicate with the Otherworlds. These thin times are celebrated on eight occasions each year. (See Appendix: The Celtic Wheel of Life.)

Calmly observing the rhythmic passages of the sun and moon, Elen understands each direction of the wheel and its purpose, including the center, where you discover yourself. Attuned with the rising sun and flying creatures, Elen can open the gateway to the east during the Spring Equinox or the eastern gate during any ceremony. East is the place of new life, birds, flying reindeer, messages from Otherworlds, ideas, birds, butterflies and new adventures. Since her totem is a deer, she can also stand at the gateway of the south, helping us with our families and careers. In the west she stands calmly as what is outdated falls away like a dry leaf. She can also listen to the ancestors of the north and bring their messages to us. Elen is specifically honored on Samhain when the veils to the Otherworld are thin.

Elen is known as the one who can protect you during your physical journeys on the roads and also your shamanic or mystical journeys to the Otherworlds. Perhaps Elen is the most ancient expression of Santa Claus, who flies with reindeer to bring presents to children. In Elen's case, her gift would probably be a message from a guide or ancestor. Elen was absorbed into western civilization as Saint Helena. Elen is as elusive as the tracks of deer, and yet as present as the forest. Elen is a guardian to call upon during times of change.

Elen In Nature
Climbing Yew Trees & Flying with Reindeer

Elen is associated with deer, particularly female reindeer which grow antlers. Her antlers represent her ability to tune into the natural world. Elen's antlers can act as mystical ears, allowing her to hear the music of the spheres.

Elen is also known as a guardian of the roads. Her path might be found on a main thoroughfare, or her roads might take you on a journey to the Otherworlds, perhaps pulled by flying reindeer. She is a skilled traveler in Celtic Underworld, Middle Earth and Upper World adventures.

Due to her ability to journey, Elen is connected to the Yew tree, one of the five sacred trees brought from the Otherworlds. It may be that the Yew was the first evergreen in Britain and therefore it was regarded as a natural symbol of everlasting life. The trees branches grow downward and form new stems, which then become new trees. *Ioho* is the letter of the Ogham that represents ancestors, death and rebirth. Yew wood has been used to carve the Ogham letters for magical use. Old Yew trees often grow in churchyards, and one way to get to know Elen is to climb into the branches of a great Yew tree. Another way to contact Elen is to become aware of and follow the tracks that deer make in the forest. You can climb Yew trees and fly with Reindeer in your imagination.

Yew Ogham

Elen's Colours
Deep Red, Green & Olive

Deep Red is the colour to use when you want to become more aware of the natural rhythm of Earth for it is the colour that helps the roots of plants grow. Green, the colour of the compassionate heart, is the most predominant colour in nature. Those of the Faery Realm love the colours Green and Deep Red, often adorning those colours. When we want to understand more about our True Nature, it is wise to take a pilgrimage in nature where we can slow down and move back into harmony and balance. It is when we give ourselves time to attune and be receptive to the natural world that magic happens. Olive is the colour of feminine empowerment, and the blessings of the Goddess of Sovereignty. Olive is the colour to use when taking a healing journey into the shadowy or more painful aspects of our being for it helps us stay on track. This combination helps us relax and trust the natural cycles of life. Thus it is known as:

"Tracking the Deer"

Meeting the Goddess Elen

When we experience deep change taking place in our lives, it is time to meet Elen. This Goddess understands how our bodies change, and she can help us understand the intelligence inherent in life, death and re-birth. Elen can also act as a guardian during Earth changes, for she hears and understands the flow of nature. Elen is present in the natural world.

You can call to Elen in the wells dedicated to Saint Helena, for there are more holy wells named after Helena in Britain than any other female saint. You can also take a pilgrimage along the Sarn Helen, a great Roman road that runs through Wales. You might find her walking along the great Ridgeway that connects Avebury in Wiltshire to Ivinghoe Beacon in Buckinghamshire.

Although her presence is strong in Britain, Elen can be felt all over the world — especially when following the tracks of deer. Or simply close your eyes and ask her to show you the way into the secrets of your own heart and soul. You might imagine for a moment that you too have sprouted antlers.

Practice
Seeing with the Eyes of a Deer

To learn to shapeshift, practice with a gentle deer. Begin by walking mindfully on the earth for at least fifteen minutes. Move slowly, as if you were a deer, moving silently and deeply in rhythm with all of life. With each step, practice listening not only with your ears, but also with your heart. Blink your eyes a few times, and then merge with the energy of the deer. Look at the woods with the deer through her eyes. As you begin to see with the eyes of a deer notice if the world around you appears differently.

Slow down, so that you can really sense what it is like to be another being. Sense your connection to the environment. Notice how your breathing changes. Try slowing down even more, so that you are barely moving. Notice that movement can be a graceful meditation and that now you can move silently through the forest. When you are ready, thank the deer for allowing you to merge with her and understand something of her medicine. Step back into your body with a renewed sense of the mysteries of life.

After you complete your seeing meditation, reflect upon the phase of life you are in now. Is there a pilgrimage you need to make, so that you can deepen your understanding? Trust that if you are listening to the wisdom of your True Nature, there are roads that will take you exactly where you need to go. Remember to stay attuned and listen carefully to the guidance that is always around you, and you will find your way.

Visualization
Growing Antlers

Imagine that snow has fallen on the ground. A full moon rises over a forest, and a silvery lunar beam casts a stream of light that is so strong you can follow it. Notice as you walk that there are deer tracks. You follow the silver beam of lunar light and the tracks until you come to three bare Ash trees whose ancient branches embrace each other forming a doorway into another world.

You pause for a moment, reflecting upon the life you have been living. Feeling the call to adventure, you step through the portal. In the moonlight, you can see a reindeer standing by a well. You walk toward her respectfully. If she allows it, you rub your head against hers. The top of your head feels oddly itchy, and so you rub harder. Soon you can feel the way in which your antlers touch Elen's. You step back, feeling for a moment what it is like to be able to hear the music of the spheres — the sound the stars make as they move through the heavens.

Elen looks at you with deep love and understanding. For a moment you can see the reflection of your physical form in her eyes. Looking down, you are drawn to the well, and peering into the dark water, you can see the moonlight casting a vision of your True Self in the water. You continue to look, amazed by the beauty of your True Nature.

When you are ready, sit back up and breathe in the freshness of the truth of who you are. There is no longer a reason to walk any path other than the one aligned with your soul. Thank Elen for her insights; she might bow in return, acknowledging the knowledge you have acquired.

Know that you can return to the well anytime you need to remember your True Self. Just pass back through the three Ash trees into this time and space. Your antlers may still be with you, although they will probably only be energetic. Before you open your eyes, touch the crown of your head and sense the sacredness of your sovereignty.

Blessings From Trees
Song of the Yew

The old Yew holds silence so the souls of the departed

Can climb her branches and listen for the starlit song

That opens the northern gateway where the ancestors feast.

There is wisdom in the passages of time.

After a loss, walk in a cemetery where branches

Scrape against gravestones gradually erasing stone effigies

And you might discover we are more than names.

Do not be afraid of climbing high into the Yew

To ask the tree to share its wisdom.

You might be surprised as an otherworldly star

Lands on your fingertips and lights up the sky

Reminding you of your eternal song of life and light,

The silver thread that connects you to the stars.

Yew Ogham

144

III
Heroines Of Avalon

ELAINE & DINDRAINE

The Grail & Ladies Of the Lake

The Lady of the Lake, the ruler of the legendary island of Avalon, is a shining and unusual sage who can mysteriously walk between worlds. She often helps Heroes or Heroines on their Grail Quests. Although she normally appears as a solitary figure, there are many Ladies of the Lake. Elaine and Dindraine — the focus of Part III — are both Ladies of the Lake.

In Arthurian legend, the Lady of the Lake offers King Arthur protection by gifting him with the magical sword, Excalibur. The Lady of the Lake is known as a semi-Divine being who exists in a universe parallel to our own. In Medieval literature, the Lady of the Lake is Argante, who raised the shining Knight of the Round Table, Sir Lancelot. In another tale, Lady of the Lake as Nimue takes Merlin's role as counselor of Camelot. Here the Lady of the Lake appears as Elaine, the lover of Lancelot and mother of Galahad, winner of the Grail. In Arthurian mythology, the Lady of the Lake consistently protects Arthur throughout his life. At his death, it is to her the sword and the King are returned. The Lady of the Lake can also be known as a Goddess of Sovereignty, who resides over the Otherworld and the land that the King inhabits and protects.

When we look through a glass prism, we see that a ray of light can divide into multiple colours. This is also true of the Lady of the Lake. The names of Elaine and Dindraine both contain some version of the Solar Goddess Aine, and they are each linked to the mysterious Land of Women, Tir Na Ban or Avalon. The High Priestess Anna is the Arthurian version of the Goddess Aine or the older Goddess Anu. The Ladies of the Lake are aspects of the Great Goddess, an ancient lineage of Light which is becoming accessible to Earth again.

Although temporarily defiled by stories of an adulterous romance involving the knight Lancelot, Guinevere is a May Queen, Goddess of Sovereignty, and a Lady of the Lake. Igraine (mother of King Arthur) is another Lady of the Lake who brings forth a son and Hero to help the evolution of humanity.

The magical isle of Avalon, also known as Tir Na Ban, and other dimensions such as Sarras, Logres and Annwn, amongst others, are realms that exist in parallel dimensions to our own. Mystics say there are portals to the Blessed Isles where initiates may be invited to enter, such as the Chalice Well or Glastonbury Tor, and other wells, hills, lakes, springs and caves, which act as mouths to the land of the Goddess. The mysterious Ladies of the Lake, including Argante and Nimue, are said to reside in Avalon even now, training those who are called to become Priestesses of the Goddess. Women visiting the ancient places of Glastonbury Tor or the Sarsen Stones of Avebury might be invited into this astral world and beyond.

During the Christianization of Britain, the many-faced Goddess was reduced to the Virgin Mary. Stories about Hag Goddesses, such as Kundry and Ragnall, were nearly forgotten. When we lose these tales, there is the danger of losing the element of our psyche that knows how to heal. When the land becomes barren and no longer supports life it is known as the Wasteland. In the darkest hour of the Wasteland, there is a cry for the Grail and the Goddess. The mysterious feminine can be silenced, hidden, burned and betrayed, but never fully lost. The Lady of the Lake has continued to haunt the imaginations of those who sense that many of the qualities and capacities of the Goddess have been lost, and that it is time, for the sake of our planet, our bodies, our psyches and our souls, to reclaim them.

The Ladies of the Lake have a long history, for the Quest for the Holy Grail is one of the most long-standing, often-told and well-known legends in Western Europe. The Grail cup appears repeatedly in the legends of the British isles in many shapes and sizes. King Bran's Cauldron of Rebirth restored warriors who had been killed in battle so they could fight again. There is also Awen, Ceridwen's Cauldron of Poetic Inspiration, that could bestow wisdom on one who sipped from it. In Celtic Christianity, the Grail or sacred cup was alleged to be at the Last Supper and the Crucifixion.

The Ladies of the Lake hold the Grail until it is time for you to discover your own Round Table, a symbol of unity and wholeness formed in the Otherworld. It has been suggested that the Quest for the Holy Grail was for the Goddess herself, who was beginning to withdraw her energy from the land and return to the Otherworlds, such as Tir Na Ban, the Land of Women, or Avalon. Some early Christian scholars claim that after Jesus rose from the dead in the Resurrection, he appeared to Joseph and gave him the Cup. They say Joseph then took the Grail to Britain, where it has been hidden and kept in secret for centuries. There are those who believe that it was concealed in the Chalice Well in Glastonbury, England, and that the ancient Goddess can still be experienced there. Some claim that the true Grail was actually the wife of Jesus, Mary Magdalene, but that is the subject of another tale. Let's turn now to the legends of our Ladies of the Lake – Elaine and Dindraine.

ELAINE

Elaine In Arthurian Legend
Goddess of Beauty & The Moon

Elaine is a personage of royal blood in line to become a queen, and her home is Castle Corbenic. There is an element of magic in her too, which suggests that she is in the lineage of Avalon, or even Tir Na Ban, the Land of Women. Elaine is generally cast as a woman who, through magic, betrays a noble knight. She appears in Arthurian legend as the one who fooled Lancelot into sleeping with her. Their union creates the shining knight Galahad, who, in some legends, eventually becomes a Grail Champion, heals Amfortas, the Fisher King, and restores the land.

Elaine is the Grail heroine who safeguards the sacred Grail cup for Lancelot and then Galahad, an act exposing her as one of the wise Ladies of the Lake. Elaine is a suitable partner for a man of Lancelot du Lac's stature. During her personal initiation into the sacred mysteries, Elaine realizes that she is not only a guardian but an embodiment of the Grail. In other words, she remembers that at the depths of her core, she is a Goddess. Elaine helps us understand that when a man is divided within himself, even the greatest love will never heal his wound. His quest is something he must undertake himself, or die trying.

Through modern eyes, Elaine is the single mother whose husband, due to his inner instability, cannot quite show up to care for his family. She is a Heroine who understands that sometimes we must quest alone, and that raising children is a noble task. Elaine is an example of a woman who fulfills her mission despite the odds. It is the shining and charismatic Lancelot who cannot recognize the gift he has been given in Elaine, and so he becomes one who struggles to succeed in his quest. He fails and goes mad for a period of time.

Mystics say that those on the spiritual quest have three choices: to go mad, die or awaken. From this perspective, we begin to see the noble hero Lancelot, lover of Guinevere, as a man who cannot reconcile the feelings within his heart. He is a man who cannot raise his son, or achieve the very dreams he seeks. The conflicted feelings he has for Elaine and Guinevere divide him against himself, and even though he touches the Grail, he cannot hold the great cup or truly embrace Elaine until he heals the division within his own nature.

The story is not over, and Lancelot still has time to mend the error of his ways. Magical Elaine heals from Lancelot's rejection, and she raises her son without the direction and guidance of a father. Although rejected, she fulfills her life purpose and mission.

Elaine is a daughter of the Fisher King Amfortas and the sister of the Grail champion Percival. Amfortas was a monarch who was wounded in the thigh or genitals by Balin, a young Knight of the Round Table. Balin was given a sword of power by a Lady of the Lake when he was too young, and in his ignorance, he killed his beloved twin brother Balan and injured the King. (In order to succeed, we each must learn to wield power correctly.) The land and the King are one, and so it is this dreadful act that counters both goodness and the continuation of life, and thus gives rise to the Wasteland. Balin's lack of judgment causes the deaths of many. Yet a Hero's or Heroine's Quest only arises when something has been lost.

Is it Elaine who betrayed Lancelot, or was it Elaine who was betrayed by those who misunderstood her? If we look at her more ancient form, we discover that Elaine's name means "Light" and that she was celebrated as a Goddess of Beauty and the Moon. We may discover in these pages that when we heal, the ending of a story changes.

The Knights Templars
& The Creation of Lancelot

I n 46 AD, a baptized disciple of Saint Mark formed a mystery school, and the followers wore a red cross, as the priests of Horus had done in Egypt. In 802 AD, an organization known as the Order of the Rose and Cross was formed. Many French kings were initiated into it. The Sufi, Essene and Cathar movements were a threat to Rome because biblical scripture was interpreted as metaphoric and initiatory to the early Gnostics.

Between the 10th and 12th centuries, a powerful order was founded that challenged the monarchies and the church. In 1118, nine men formed the Knights Templar Order with the mission to protect pilgrims on the way from Europe to Jerusalem, the Holy Land. The Knights Templars had been taught by Sufis, Druids and Cathars, as well as Qabbalists, and they were concerned with tracking down and preserving sacred documents. After the French Cathars were wiped out in a Crusade by Pope Innocent III, the Knights Templars knew that their existence rested on the ability to remain amicable with the Catholic Church.

In the 12th Century, King Henry II of England and Eleanor of Aquitaine were fascinated by the legends of King Arthur, and even named a grandson Arthur. The Queen loved performances of romances and mystery plays. As the literature of courtly love developed, stories arose in which a knight would commit himself to a married woman. Through heroic service, he would attempt to win the lady's heart. Adultery was not permitted, but there is a suggestion that the knight would sometimes win more than her heart.

Eleanor supported an early Renaissance to flourish in her court, in which traveling poets and singers (known as Troubadours) became increasingly popular. Although they were largely fictional, the Arthurian legends were told and retold by poets as histories. Henry II was so concerned about the "Return of the Once & Future King" that he had a chieftain's bones (thought to be Arthur's) dug up and moved to Glastonbury Abbey with great ceremony.

Eleanor of Aquitaine was particularly fond of the story of Tristan and Yseult. It is rumored that Eleanor, who was the wife first of Louis VII of France and then Henry II of England, may have been the inspiration behind the story of Guinevere. As the stories spread in popularity throughout Christendom, which included Constantinople and Alexandria, it became fashionable for people to visit the sites associated with Arthur—such as the Isle of Avalon or Glastonbury in Somerset, and Caerleon on the River Usk in Wales.

The Knights Templars gathered great mysteries in the Holy Lands that they brought back to France. In the beginning, they were known as the saviors of humanity. However, they also discovered something known as "the great secret" that may have threatened the existence of the Roman Catholic Church and the monarchy. The lands and wealth of the Knights Templars were confiscated. History states that the Knights Templar Order was completely suppressed in 1307 with the execution of its last Grand Master, Jacques de Molai, who was burned at the stake in front of Notre Dame in Paris. Although 619 Templars were executed, they were the brave few who stayed and sacrificed themselves, while approximately eighteen ships sailed, taking the wealth, documents and treasures to new places. Many fled to Scotland where they supported King Robert the Bruce's fight for independence. They eventually became known as the Freemasons. Those in the lineage of the Knights Templar continue to safeguard the alchemical secrets of the Holy Grail.

Lancelot

Like King Arthur and the Knights of the Round Table, the role of the Knight Templars was to protect the sacred and serve God first. They lived under the will of God (the Great Architect of the Universe) and strove to find the Sacred Light that burned within. The Templars realized that the true battle was not about fight or flight, but transformation of themselves. Once they found the Light or the Grail, they then acted as alchemists, transmuting the pain and suffering of the world. The rose is a symbol of everlasting life and love, and is also discretely feminine by design.

The mythos that arose out of the Knights Templar tradition was that the Grail or sacred cup was at the Last Supper, and then present during the Crucifixion, where it was held up to receive blood flowing from Christ's side. Due to His blood, the Holy Grail was thought to have special healing and alchemical powers.

The Myth
Of Lancelot
The Most Loved Knight

eoffrey of Monmouth (1100-1155) was a Welsh cleric who is known for his collection of Celtic legends, *Historia Regum Britanniae,* which was the first popular recording of Arthurian myth. The stories were wildly successful in Britain until the 16th century. The 12th century poet Chretien de Troyes developed the Arthurian legends and originated Lancelot. There is no accident that the world of Lancelot and King Arthur bears resemblance to that of the original Knights Templars. Chretien of Troyes' cousin was Catherine de St. Clair, who was the wife of the first Grand Master of the Templar Order, Hugues de Payens. Bernard of Clairvaux (a thin ascetic who knew Eleanor of Aquitaine and taught that God was a benevolent and loving father) learned of Gnostic traditions from his uncle, who was one of the original founders of the Knights Templar Order. He was also the order's fifth Grand Master. These original knights came from Cathar families who valued and taught Gnostic wisdom. It was Chretien de Troyes, as well as the medieval poet Marie de France, who developed Arthur into the ideal king and Lancelot into the most loved knight.

Lancelot du Lac's name (*du lac* can be translated as "from the lake") suggests a close relationship with the Ladies of the Lake, whose fate he is intertwined with. His father was the French King Ban of Banoic (in Welsh legend, he was Pant of Genewis) and his mother or foster-mother is a Lady of the Lake. His sword is called "Secace" but as his name implies, it is the lance (spear or magical wand) that is his true gift. In Lancelot's special case, this translates into him possessing the ability to see into Otherworlds. It is this quality of penetration that made him irresistible to women.

Drawn by stories of Camelot, Lancelot became a knight of the Round Table, and he proved to be the most fearless, handsome and valiant of knights. Lancelot liked to travel in disguise, and the knight used different armor and shields as weapons. In the Vulgate Cycle, he is knighted as a White Knight, with a Lady of the Lake giving him weapons. Later he is knighted as a Red, Green and then a Black Knight, which might suggest levels of initiations in a secret order or mystery school.

While Lancelot is best known for the fatal love triangle with King Arthur and Guinevere, his legend is also entwined with the tragic Elaine. This young maiden, who loved Lancelot, is rejected, and then perishes from a broken heart. In the tale of Elaine of Astolat, King Arthur, Queen Guinevere, Lancelot and other knights see a barge carrying Elaine's lifeless body. King Arthur slips a note out of the maiden's hand. It expresses her love for Lancelot and asks all women for pity. The valiant knight covers his face and weeps.

As we remember the form of Elaine, let's unbind her from the laws of courtly love. It's time for Elaine and Lancelot's story to be re-told so that the energies of misunderstanding, madness and suicide are healed, and a new legend may arise—one of inner light, wisdom and empowerment.

Elaine's Untold Story
Guardian of the Grail

From the first moment I met Dame Brisden, I found her to be magical. She knew all the herbs that grew along the meadows and the songs they made. At night, she gathered roots under the guidance of the moonlight and took them inside to warm them on shelves by the hearth. The pulses of the plants guided her to a mastery of herbal medicine. She was one of the old ones who understood Nature, a tradition that has been largely lost by rough boots and insensitivity. For those who listen to the flow of life, violence and domination are anathema.

My beloved father, Amfortas, was stabbed by a boy named Balin, who had not understood the power of his sword. The wound would not heal, and throughout my childhood at Castle Corbenic, my father called out in pain. Dame Brisden helped him somewhat, but we all knew the only one who could heal the King was a knight who carried a magical sword with grace and wisdom. The wound was made by a man and needed to be healed by a man. My mother, disillusioned by knights in shining armor, had gone away into the forest with my young brother, Percival, hoping he would choose another path. She could have just as well stayed with me and enjoyed having a daughter, because there is no way a parent can make children choose any path other than the one that calls to them.

As Merlin became a guide for young Arthur, Dame Brisden became my foster mother. She never told me about her parents or her training, for in those times it was not safe to be anything but Christian. I felt that she had been raised amongst Druids, for she knew the secrets of the trees and how to weave spells, although she never admitted as much. When I was young, she taught me to tie a red thread around my left wrist for protection. Dame Brisden told me that it would keep me from taking in negativity from the outside world. She forgot to tell me that those who play with healing and magic can sometimes find themselves mired in trouble.

One spring afternoon when the sun was high overhead, I decided to study the lilies that were blossoming at a natural pond. This small body of water arose from a warm spring in the land of Listenois just outside Castle Corbenic, which was my home. I went alone, not expecting to be seen.

Yellow water lilies were blooming on the surface of the pond, so I laid my dress neatly on a tree stump and walked into the water. I observed the ferns growing along the high banks of the pool, just unfurling in the dappled light, and the way in which the new leaves and branches of the weeping willows trailed into the water.

Dame Brisden was teaching me about the Doctrine of Signatures, a way of reading a plant's medicine by observing not only its scent, but also its colour, shape and the feeling that would arise within while viewing it. This practice came under harsh criticism from the priests, but I always found it to have an uncanny precision. Although Brisden thought it unwise, I preferred to view plants in the midday when the sun was most brilliant. While observing the lilies that had opened fully in the water, I noticed a sound they made and began humming it to myself.

That's when I noticed that there was a silver-haired woman floating just under the surface of the water, and she was looking at me. At first I was frightened by her, but she was surrounded by a bright light and I was drawn to her mystery. She rose up out of the pool slowly, revealing a radiant beauty, until she was half out of the water. I noticed that her hair seemed dry, even though she had been below the surface of the water only moments before.

The Lady of the Lake was tall and slender with a long yet lovely pale face. She wore a necklace made of shimmering seashells and looked at me with startling emerald-green eyes.

"I am Argante," she said with her mind. "I have been sent to bring you both a gift and a test."

The Lady of the Lake held up a flat and well-polished black obsidian stone that was almost the size of her palm. I felt that she wanted me to look into it, and so I did. In this way, the Lady of the Lake opened me up to a visionary realm that I had not been invited into before.

Looking into the polished surface of the gemstone, I had a vision of myself in a pool surrounded by white fire. I saw the water steaming, a man carrying me out, a child, and my father healing. It was clear to me that it was necessary to undertake a purification ritual that would test me severely.

Slowly she brought a small golden cup up out of the water and held it above her head, where it shimmered in the sunlight. Clearly both Goddess and Grail had emerged from an Otherworld from which the Light of the Christos flowed into my shaking form.

The Lady of the Lake had not finished bringing me both aspiration and visions. Argante came so close that her silver hair brushed against my face, which made me shiver. As she brought the Grail toward me, I was mesmerized and reached out for it with my right hand. Argante pushed me back sharply with a long and lovely white hand. It was partly covered in a translucent glove that looked like silver fish scales, possibly created by the artists of Tir Na Ban.

"Use your left hand, for that is the wrist where Dame Brisden has placed the Red Thread of Pass Me Not. It is also the hand that receives energies," she said in my mind. "The Grail will not harm you, but it could kill the uninitiated."

I was slightly startled when Argante brought the Grail toward me and motioned for me to drink. At first I was not certain that I should touch it, yet when it came close to me I grasped the cup and held it firmly in my left hand. The cup's contents sparkled with golden light and seemed more like fire than liquid. I brought it to my lips and for a moment white flames tickled my mouth. A white fire flowed from the vessel into me and it tasted so sweet, I thought perhaps it was ambrosia. Immediately I began to feel incredible peace. The love of the Otherworlds flowed into and awakened my heart. I laughed aloud.

The Lady of the Lake played with me, showing how she could move the cup across the surface of the water with her thoughts, or even raise it into the air like a small firebird. I also began to play with the golden cup in this way. The Grail responded to me and moved accordingly.

"The Grail serves Thee," whispered Argante.

Feeling healed by its light, I held out the golden cup so that the Lady could take it back to the world from which it came. But she simply stared at me and motioned for me to sip yet again. Although she did not speak, I knew what the Lady of the Lake wanted of me. It was my turn to tend the cup for a while. I knew in that moment that I was to be its guardian until the one it was meant for appeared.

I began to feel weak at the knees, and I thought for a moment of turning away. All around me there were golden birds with red beaks that sang sweet melodies. Surrendering to my fate, I almost sank into the depths of the water. But I would not have found my way to the magical land of women, Tir-Na Ban, at that time. My path had not been prepared and I was not ready to make that journey, because my assignment was to stay fully embodied and on this earth. The Lady of the Lake had not come to take me to an Otherworld. Instead she was there to remind me that pools, rivers, wells and springs are the abode of the Goddess and what I held was the Holy Grail.

I wondered why I had been given the cup of white fire and what my role was as its guardian. She must have sensed my questions for Argante came close and her presence illuminated the water. Looking down, I saw dark creatures who wished to enter the pool being held back by the power of the Grail that was now in my care.

At that moment, I felt a serpent wrap itself around my right thigh, and I shrieked, "Get it off!"

The golden cup became so luminous that I had to look away. Looking down I saw a large eel dart backwards as if stung and then slide into a cave beneath the bank of the pool.

"Elaine of Corbenic," I heard the Lady of the Lake say inside my mind. "There are many things living beneath the surface that we pretend not to know. Do you accept the test? Will you carry the Grail that few may hold without perishing?"

I brought the luminous Grail beneath the water and held it against my breasts. After a few moments I felt heat in the pool, as though the white fire that burned within the Grail could bring the water to a boil. Yet at the same time, a Light from within my own heart and belly aligned with the Light from the golden cup, and I was not harmed by its intensity.

"You are the one," I heard Argante say silently.

"I choose to be a Grail Guardian," I told her. I do not remember thinking the words, they just flowed through my lips. I thought of Arthur pulling the sword from the stone, and the sword given to him by the Lady of the Lake. It was not a weapon that Argante was giving me, but a cup of life that seemed to hold the potency of the world.

I brought the Grail out of the water and peered at it carefully. The surface was polished and gleamed with gold, but when I gazed inside the Grail the colour could change. At first it was golden, then the liquid turned black, like the endless nighttime sky at a time when the stars shine brightly. Usually its surface burned with a white fire that was brighter than the sun. Yet the Grail did not burn my flesh, but seemed to want to be a part of my body.

I felt a hot sensation run through my arm, and there was a flash of Light. My sense of self vanished, and I was no longer Elaine but the Goddess. Immediately, the love I had for the world was so vast that I felt I could embrace all men and women, and all of its other sentient creatures. My tears fell into the pool, like diamonds into Light. I had been chosen by the Goddess to be an embodiment of the Grail, a treasure that was sought by many.

Argante's words formed as whispers in my thoughts: "Every force on Earth will try to destroy you. No matter what, be the Grail until the time that a worthy knight comes. You will know him because the waters will cool at his touch. Your union will produce a child that will be a Light upon this world. I will return to you at that time and help you raise the new and future king."

Argante descended quickly into the water, and like a fish darting into the shadows, she was gone. Only a few ripples suggested that the Lady had ever visited me, and, of course, there was the golden cup that I now held, or perhaps it held me. The Grail shone with such vigor that it seemed as though a piece of the sun had come to Earth. I was mesmerized by it, and I felt my own body beginning to dissolve into Light.

"What have you done?" I heard Dame Brisden call out a short time later.

"It's the Grail," I responded, holding it out towards her. "I am a Guardian of the Grail. The Red Thread protected me!"

Dame Brisden shielded her eyes from the brilliancy of the cup. "It's a heavy burden," she noted. "Toss it to shore and into my care. You do not have enough knowledge in you yet to carry that much Light."

It was too late, for the serpents that live in the underwater caves and along the banks of the pond came, and they began to swim around me in a counter-clockwise circle. They created a vacuum, and I felt that I was being pulled downwards.

"I will boil them alive!" yelled Brisden, who began chanting in a tongue that sounded like Elfin. *"Brauel el licht, ni glaum das shee…"*

The water boiled and steam covered the pool. Like white fire, the hot swirling waters burned everything they touched, except the stones and myself, Guardian of the Grail. Then, for five years, the waters swirled. Shades and shadows haunted me, tried to seduce and suck my life force from me, yet never once was the Grail out of my grasp. For safekeeping, I often held it between my thighs or wove it into my hair. There was little eating, apart from the flowers and herbs that Brisden gave me. I did not sleep nor did I awaken in all that time. There was no reprieve from the onslaught of torment, but for the ambrosia that would flow at times like a white fire from the cup. There were times when I felt divided against myself, but the Grail was my salvation and the wildness in me would flow away. The Light never left me; it was my grace, for without it I would have been lost forever.

Forms arose from the pool that offered me great riches, fame, fortune and even enduring love in exchange for the cup. I knew of the diamond light it contained, and I could never be separated from the Grail without the world going dark. So I never gave into any seduction.

All that time Brisden stayed by my side, cooling me when she could, offering me fruit and leaves that I rarely ate. I grew thin and pale, almost a Light myself.

"Don't die," Brisden counseled me. "You are the Grail now. You have become the Light, and from you can be born an even greater Light. Men and women together weave a land that flourishes. If they separate, then all is bleak."

As we watched, a Kingfisher dove into the pool and carried away one of the eels. It was a symbol to me that my rescuer was coming.

One day a man carrying a sword made of silver walked down the barren rocks that had become a staircase to my doom. I wondered if this was the man who had come to win my most precious possession. He could not see me in the mad swimming of Light and Dark, so I pulled the Grail below the surface of the boiling pool and placed it firmly between my thighs where I held it tight. He walked into the steaming waters, which cooled at his touch. It was clear that he was one of the shining ones, and it was he who would set me free and take me to my destiny.

When he touched me, his fingers blistered and his eyes grew red and inflamed, for I was the Light.

Afraid I would harm him, I asked, "What do you seek?"

He answered, "The Lady of the Lake has sent me on a mission to find the Holy Grail."

I relaxed then, for I knew I had passed the test. As we spoke, my body and the waters became so cool, that for the first time in five years I felt a chill. It seemed that his touch changed me from a hot afternoon sun to a crescent moon.

Lancelot lifted my body from the waters and I relaxed into his great arms. He then sniffed me, as though smelling nectar, and kissed my hair. Clearly, he was a man who responded naturally to the gifts of the Grail. Quickly I pulled the cup into my long hair, and although he stepped back from the Light of it for an instant, he still held me firm.

Once on land, he set me down and I exposed the Grail. It shimmered as if in reaction to the knight. Lancelot, realizing that he was before the great golden cup, knelt at my feet and wept. Slowly he reached up to touch the Grail. It glowed so brightly that he covered his eyes and withdrew his hand. He did not take the cup, but let it stay with me as he picked me up in his arms.

"The cup is yours, my lady," he said. "For you are the Grail and the secret that all men seek."

Brisden tried to block us, but the passion was too strong, and Lancelot swept past her as though she were an autumn leaf. The Grail acted as a love potion that drew us together in a way that could not be stopped. As soon as he kissed me, my body mended and regained its vigor. In some ways, Lancelot was my healer. We needed each other to feel whole.

Lancelot had no other queen in his mind as he carried me to my bed. The Light from the cup dazzled him, but it was also our destiny to become one. His lips and my lips became one lake through which we poured our bodies, souls and spirits. The Grail showed us the ecstasy of union. It was not one night but many that we lay together. Dame Brisden insisted that we be married in a church by a Celtic priest, but the vows had little meaning for Lancelot. When a seed took root in my womb, our time together was done. Although I wished it could have been otherwise, I felt Lancelot's mind wander to another queen.

We both knew that our togetherness had brought forth a new king. When Lancelot began to withdraw from me, I thought my heart would break. It was as if an earthquake tore apart our worlds. Perhaps it was not time on Earth for us to live as one, and so we broke apart like a mighty diamond splitting into two slivers that must always seek one another. The next morning, he was gone.

I thought the loneliness would kill me, and I cried longer and louder than I ever had in the boiling pool. But Lancelot could no longer hear me. The totality of our union had been as complete as the darkness and sadness of our separation was now. When Lancelot withdrew from me, he began to experience madness.

As I had spent five years in the boiling pool, Lancelot spent seven years as a tangled-haired beggar running in the forest. Although he tried, the knight could not find salvation in any woman, even the May Queen Guinevere, for he had lost his way. I suffered, knowing that he cried out night after night in sorrow and in pain. I still held the very cup the sought, and as the days moved on, the Grail and I became one entity.

I did not know whose injury was worse, my father's or my husband's. Both carried wounds that would not heal. Many times I found Lancelot sleeping in the nearby woods and tried to bring my body close to him, but he no longer recognized me and would run away like a frightened animal. If only he had touched me, his sanity would have been restored. I was the Grail he sought.

Brisden was with me when I birthed my son. He was not to have the presence of a father, but Galahad was born whole within himself.

He needed little beyond the food, clothing and shelter required of any mortal. Castle Corbenic shielded him, and as Galahad grew, I noticed he carried wisdom beyond his years. Brisden took him under her wing, and eventually Argante came back and explained that Galahad had been born without a blemish, which is rare amongst men and women.

When it was time to present our son at Camelot, I sent a messenger to announce our arrival. Perhaps Guinevere's divided love had confused her womb too much to conceive, or perhaps it was simply my fate to bring forth the new king. We went to Camelot accompanied by 50 ladies and 50 knights, as befits a queen, as well as my brother, Sir Percival, and another knight, Sir Bors.

Bors had asked for my hand in marriage and I had thanked him. However, I knew that I must continue to love my son Galahad with a pure heart and mind, so that he could be the champion he was destined to be. The Grail Light can shatter our mind if we are not ready, or heal us and makes us whole when we are prepared. Lancelot had been driven mad by the quest for the Grail, and he was not the only one. The first time Percival saw the Holy Grail he was so dazzled by the Light that he had forgotten to ask questions about the wounded king and failed the quest. He learned from his mistakes and eventually achieved the Grail, which is the subject of another tale. I knew the Grail had become an integral part of who I was as a woman and champion. I was the cup and had no need to carry it.

During our journey, I felt compelled to cut my long hair that ran freely to my ankles. I was no longer a maiden, but had a new role to play. I borrowed Balin's sword and sliced the hair off at my shoulders. In doing so, I was freeing myself of the story of pain and suffering that I had been carrying. I needed to release Lancelot and all tragedy from my life. I had no interest in being a victim or an object of pity, and so I wiped my life clean. Afterwards, I braided a new story into my hair, along with lilies and prayers. Brisden watched as I crafted a soft girdle for Galahad to wear so that he could sit on any seat or throne and serve miraculously unharmed by a sorcerer's magic. As it was with his parents, fire and heat could not harm Galahad, but instead the flames would cool to a gentle warmth at his touch.

When we arrived at Camelot, I was greeted first by Queen Guinevere, who looked at me as though I were a sister. She carried such great love that all hearts could be healed by the sight of her, with one exception, our Lancelot. I understood immediately how she could love both a king and a knight, for in truth as May Queen her heart was so great that she was capable of loving the entire world. She embraced me, and then Galahad, who she held long and tight. Perhaps she felt Lancelot in him. She looked at Galahad, who radiated goodness, and nodded, acknowledging the place he had come to take at the Round Table.

King Arthur had been seated as we entered the great room, and all knights were silent as Galahad unfastened his red cape and walked to the vacant chair.

"That seat is perilous," warned the King. "It is reserved for the finest knight in the world, and all others who attempt it perish. Choose wisely before taking your seat, for you seem like a fine young man."

Galahad knew his place. He walked past Merlin, who had designed the chair for precisely the purpose the King had described. Without hesitating, my son took the seat that had long awaited him. All watched to see if he would be consumed by fire, but I had already suffered that fate for him in the white fire of the pool and lived. My womb and my son were polished by flames, not harmed by them. Galahad looked around at those staring at him and laughed in such a delightful way that all in his presence joined in the merriment. I need not have woven a girdle for him after all, for I realized Galahad was protected by his own goodness and his lineage of Divine Light. A flock of white doves landed near the table and listened while inspired musicians played melodies given to them from the Otherworlds.

I walked to his side to congratulate Galahad, but he stood suddenly and offered the chair to me and bowed. No woman other than Guinevere had sat amongst Arthur and his knights. After all, it was her table. Silence filled the room and Guinevere looked on with great curiosity.

Galahad looked at me and said intently, "Mother, the knights all went in search of the Grail, that very thing you held in your hair and against your body until it became a part of you. You are the Grail men seek."

"The Grail is part of all women, and certain radiantly beautiful men," I said, smiling at my son. "It will come to each of us in a way that is unique. The Grail is always mysterious, and reminds us of the greater mysteries of our own essence. If the Grail shows itself to you, remember to serve the Light well."

"The Grail is the Light that lives within you, Mother," Galahad insisted. "You taught me so, and if I am the Light, then you must also be. We are here to serve the Light within everyone."

For a moment I hesitated, thinking of the boiling pool and Lancelot's madness. I did not wish to undergo another test. If I burst into flames, what would become of my son?

"It is your seat," persisted Galahad. "The one missing is the Goddess."

"He speaks the Truth," declared Guinevere. "When the Goddess returns, the land shall flourish and all will heal."

"Let's sit in the chair together," I replied at last.

Galahad took my hand, and it seemed as though the chair grew wide, to hold us both. We sat together, although not quite in the way I had expected. The late afternoon sun made its way through a high window, and the room became illuminated. Guinevere took Arthur's hand and they also sat together. So much love filled the room that several other ladies joined their sons and husbands. The sorrow felt for those who had been lost on the Quest dissolved into the shared care we felt for one another. The men and women who now sat at the table rejoiced.

"We are one at my table now!" sang Guinevere. "May peace, prosperity, fertility and love reign on Earth forever."

Galahad stood up abruptly. Tall and silvery Argante had entered the room, and as she spoke, a Golden Chalice descended from the high ceiling of the castle. My son stepped onto the arm of the chair and then onto the Round Table. A Golden Star arose out of the Holy Grail, and it traveled downwards, resting just above Galahad's fair head. His body began to glow with radiant light. Galahad blinked, then his head fell back and his body shuddered with Divine Ecstasy.

"The Christ is here," he said, as though looking through the Star into another world. Perhaps he saw Sarras, for Heaven seemed to be calling him. We all heard celestial music.

Galahad paused for a moment and, with an ecstatic smile, turned and looked lovingly at each one of us. Then he touched the Golden Star and pulled a ray of Light into his heart. At that instant, the

Divine Light took him. Galahad smiled sweetly as he was transported skyward by angels. He glanced at me for a moment and so great was his bliss that I reached toward him. I was shocked and yet delighted that my son had died to this world in order to reign as King in Sarras. I wished to follow him, but a hand pulled me back. I turned to see Lancelot, radiant in his wholeness.

"Stay with me," he urged. "Our task is done. Let us enjoy our last years together in this earthly kingdom."

Guinevere smiled generously, and even Arthur looked at me with some curiosity. I laughed and soon all the knights and ladies of the Round Table joined us in our merriment.

"I do not know whether we are now in heavenly Sarras or if we still exist on Earth," I responded to him. "What I do know is that I wish to spend the rest of my years loving you." Then looking around the room, I added, "Loving all of you."

Holding a sword that shimmered in the fading sunlight, Lancelot said, "I will return Balin's sword of power to your father now."

I knew then that the Lady of the Lake had healed the Fisher King and that my father was now well. As the days grew into years and the land flourished once again, all that mattered was that we lived life completely and fully together—as it was meant to be.

Honoring Elaine

Celebrating Elaine
A Lineage of Light

Elaine and the magical Ladies of the Lake can be called upon to open the western gateway of the Celtic Wheel of Life on Mabon. They remind us that although we are constantly changing forms, our essence never dies. Elaine's name includes Aine, a Goddess of the Sun, which hints at her light-filled origin. Elaine's name means "Light." The Lily Maid Elaine is specifically honored each year on October 6 as the Goddess of Beauty and the Moon.

Elaine, Lillake & Lillith

There are some mystics who whisper that Elaine is a daughter of the Egyptian Goddess Isis, and has received her healing gifts. Others claim that she is in the lineage of Lilith, who appears in Judeo-Christian legend as the first wife of Adam, before Eve. There is a story told by theosophists in which Lilith and Adam are described as twins, both created equally out of the clay of the soil and the breath of the Divine. A fiery, passionate and independent Mother Goddess, Lilith is clearly Adam's equal. Because she refuses to listen to Adam, she is expelled from the Garden of Eden and becomes a Queen of the Night. It is said that she took the form of a serpent and dwells within the forces of darkness. Some say she was the snake that tempted Eve. In order to frighten women into subservience, in the 10th century Lilith was demonized. It is time for us to look at the story more carefully, for perhaps it was Lilith who gave us self-knowing. We find can find the shadow-archetype

182

of Lilith within ourselves when a relationship has become difficult and we no longer have the gentleness to listen or bend.

Lilith thinks for herself. She is not going to settle and behave in a man's world, because she has her own work to do. She will not be labeled as a wife. Lilith knows that she is part of the totality of existence, and she does not want to be limited or confined by definitions. She is brave, daring and interested in her own evolution. Lilith is strong enough to live alone without the help of a man, and she wants to know who she is as separate from God. In this century, Lilith would be considered more of a Heroine. In fact now the Lilith archetype seems alive and well in many western women.

Once the mystery around Lilith begins to dissolve, we see that it is likely that she is in the lineage of the Goddess Isis, one of the most important Deities of ancient Egypt. The Goddess Isis is a lover, mother and healer, who also raised her son alone.

Although Lilith is definitely disliked by the patriarchy, she is loved by feminists and anyone interested in learning the origins of Her-Story. She encourages us to become rebellious and to live our life in our own creative way. Having a mind of her own, Lilith enjoys sexual experimentation and freedom. She understands the eternal wheel of life and re-birth, and is therefore not afraid of illness or death. Although often cursed for it, she will help as someone crosses beyond the veil. Wild, magical and orgiastic, Lilith is the type of woman that men both fear and long for. She is free. Her greatest gift is her ability to destroy what is false within us.

Once we remove layers of misogyny, we can see that Lilith is neither good nor evil. She does not reside in the realm of duality, but as a representation of the Totality of the universe. Lilith, when infuriated, can be a vengeful witch, but she is also strong, nurturing, responsible and self-sustaining. Lilith is the empowered feminine.

Another name for Lilith is Lillake. There are elements of Lilith that can be recognized in all the powerful and mysterious Ladies of the Lake, particularly Elaine who must raise her child alone. Each one of us can tap into the Great Mother Goddess and find the sustenance, intelligence and strength to live fully and completely into each moment.

The key is that we are neither good nor evil, we are neither shadow nor divine light, we are neither successes nor failures. We are all of this and more. We achieve the Grail when we realize we are a spark of the loving wisdom that creates the universe. We are an integral part of all that is.

Elaine In Nature
Willows, Doves & Lilies

Elaine's tree is the Willow, which is often found growing along the edge of the flowing water. Its bark is known to ease pain and suffering, and perhaps Dame Brisden administered it to Elaine to help her through her five-year initiation as a Grail Maiden. A sacred tree of the Druids, the Willow teaches us to bend with the winds so we do not break. According to Druidic tradition, two sacred serpent eggs hatched beneath the great Willow giving birth to humankind. The Ogham for Willow, *Saille*, is used for understanding the Dream Time, and developing clairvoyance. Doves love Willow trees, and sometimes visit to remind us to learn to cooperate and build a loving community in which all can thrive. When a dove visits us, it is a reminder to attune with spirit and develop inner peace. Elaine can also be the Dove of Peace. Her flower is the Lily, which as an essence evokes the soul of the feminine. The Lily is the Grail cup of the flower kingdom.

Lancelot In Nature
Kingfishers, Eels & Vines

As a totem bird, the Kingfisher reminds us to be patient so that we can open to a higher spiritual perspective. His bill is dagger-like and when hunting his timing is precise. Ultimately the Kingfisher can dive deep into rich pools of emotion and teach us right relationship to life.

Eels as totem animals are magical and often appear in folklore as shape-shifters. In some tales eels grow legs and walk on land. They are always connected to sexuality and spiritual transformation. When an eel visits it is usually time for a quest.

In the Ogham for the Vine is *Muin*. Vines such as blackberry and grape are often celebrated during the harvest festivals. Vines remind us to overcome our selfish tendencies and open to the creative flow inherent in nature. Vine reminds us to plan celebrations, gather with friends and families, and to love life exactly the way it is.

Elaine's Colours
Turquoise, Red & Yellow

Elaine's three sacred colours are Turquoise, Red and Yellow. Turquoise is the colour of playfulness, creativity and communication with the feeling side of our being. It helps us stay attuned to nature spirits and ancient wisdom. A Goddess who radiates Turquoise light can adapt to almost any situation, for it is a color of the Higher Heart.

During her years in the boiling pool, Elaine is forced to embody the Red essence of strength so that she can endure her ordeal. She does survive and is stronger for the initiation. With the higher vibrations of the Turquoise, and the grounding aspects of the Red, you might find that you can create your way into and out of any set of circumstances and blossom like a Lily. When we trust the wisdom of our Higher Heart and the timing of the Goddess, all things are possible.

Naturally intelligent and independent, Elaine shines in her own unique way. Her essential quality of Yellow reminds us of her innate brilliance and she is unapologetic in the ways in which she shines. Her Yellow essence helps her overcome fear and stay curious throughout her ordeal. This triple combination is known as:

"The Initiate"

Lancelot's Colours
Green, Red & Silver or Grey

Lancelot's sacred colours are Green, Red and Silver or Grey. This combination is called "Breaking Free" for it reminds us that we can always choose to live life in a new way. Green is the colour of the compassionate heart that loves nature and is a natural lover. Red is the colour of passion and the strength that it takes to be a Grail Champion. Red and Green together is a combination loved by Fairy-folk and reminds us of Lancelot's upbringing by the Ladies of the Lake. Silver is the colour that links us back to our starry origins. Grey is the colour of armor and weapons of war; it is a colour that helps us integrate sanity and restores self-esteem.

"Breaking Free"

Meeting The Heroine Elaine

We have a Divine right to defend ourselves if we are ever threatened with any type of harm. If we have found ourselves in a situation that we are not sure we can endure, it is time to meet the Heroine Elaine. This Lily maiden has the ability to gently survive the most stressful initiations. Also be practical and stay attuned to your own guidance. Make any sensible changes that need to be made in your life.

Dame Brisden, one of the magical women of Tir Na Ban, knew that Elaine would face the test presented to all Grail Champions. So she taught her the practice of the Red Thread. A thread itself is thin and can easily break. But when you call upon your Higher Self and the Magical Women of Tir Na Ban to assist you, an energetic red thread surrounds you like a protective bubble. This practice appears in many ancient traditions.

189

Elaine also reminds you to question the story you tell about your life and the people who are close to you. At any moment you may choose to awaken from dramas and nightmares, and live a new life full of the glories of the present moment. Elaine's message is that of self-care.

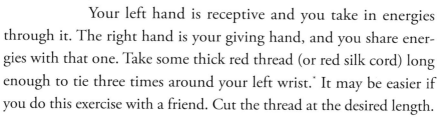

Practice
The Red Thread of Pass Me Not

You will need:

Red thread or red silk cord

Scissors or a knife to cut the thread/cord

Your left hand is receptive and you take in energies through it. The right hand is your giving hand, and you share energies with that one. Take some thick red thread (or red silk cord) long enough to tie three times around your left wrist.* It may be easier if you do this exercise with a friend. Cut the thread at the desired length.

Holding the red thread in your hands, call upon the immortal Lily Goddess Elaine to lead you away from harm, and to guide and protect you now and always. Then take the thread and wrap it around your wrist one time. If it feels correct to you, ask that Elaine and the women of Tir Na Ban teach you through dreams and visions how to discover the Grail of Light that resides in your own body, heart, mind and soul.

Now wrap the red thread a second time, and using the words that feel right to you, claim the Divine Light that resides within you as your strength and protection. Wrap the red thread a third time in honor of your own body, mind and soul. Close your eyes and with your inner sight imagine that there is a labyrinth or mandala of protection that is now around your body keeping you safe, healthy and out of harm's way. Feel the sensations in your body as shields of protection are granted to you.

---

* Some people prefer having the cord tied around their left ankle, which is just as good.

You can state aloud, "This Red Thread of Pass Me Not is a symbol of my Divine protection. I ask the Infinite Light to be with me always. May I live in right relationship with all life."

Wear the Red Thread of Pass Me Not at all times until the thread naturally falls away over days or weeks. The more you imagine the sphere of protection around yourself and the more diligent you are about staying aligned with the Light, the more powerful the practice will be.

Visualization
Daring to Be Free

Elaine does a magnificent job of "keeping her head together" even when surrounded by challenges. Having basic trust, Elaine knows that wherever she is in life and whatever circumstances she finds herself embroiled in are perfect for her optimal growth and actualization. Trapped for five years in a boiling pool, Elaine must rely on her soul's understanding of her situation. Five is the number of independence and daring. It is also the number of points on a pentagram, representing the five elements: Fire, Earth, Water, Air and Spirit.

Elaine must rely on her inner guidance as she remains confined until rescued by Lancelot, and then she soon finds herself once again limited by pregnancy. In addition, she is given the task of raising their son on her own. The lovely thing about Elaine is that she is never a victim or a martyr. Elaine knows that she is a Goddess and faces life head-on. The presence of wise Dame Brisden helps, but in order to free herself and Lancelot from an outdated love triangle, she must persevere with what she feels is good, noble and true. With her strong and positive outlook on life, there is no way Elaine can fail. With a mother like Elaine, her son Galahad is destined to become the greatest of Grail Champions.

Trapped, misunderstood and betrayed, Elaine claims her role as a Goddess of Sovereignty. It is then—and only then—that her life changes and the lives of those close to her. She is a true Goddess and Heroine of the highest order.

Imagine a situation in your life right now where you feel limited, confined, puzzled or even trapped. Visualize it fully. Do not be afraid of being present to the difficulty of the situation. Call Elaine to you and ask her to help you stand completely and effectively in the truth of who you are. Feel how the presence of Elaine strengthens your body. You might feel the red strength essence opening within you. Know that you have what it takes to endure and learn from the situation.

You may then feel a pulsation in your brow (or another part of your body) as your golden yellow Light of Inner Guidance opens up. Listen carefully to the signs and the messages the Goddess is

194

bringing you. In this moment, you are linked to a greater intelligence that knows what your soul needs to learn and what the gift of the challenge truly is. In Elaine's case, she needed to experience herself as independent, strong and sovereign. Once she really accepted her lesson, Elaine's life changed.

What is it you are learning right now? Be willing to drop all blame and judgment. Stand in the boiling pool of transformation and increased awareness. Awaken to the truth of who you are without fear. Trust the process of life.

Elaine's colour combination of turquoise, red and yellow helps us stay centered in the higher heart, firm in bodily awareness, and connected to the intelligence of Self. Realize the situation is temporary, and thank the Goddess and all people who have volunteered to be players in your life. Free yourself by dropping all blame, victimization, guilt and shame into the boiling pool, and step out awakened, strong and free. What is the treasure you are receiving now? Thank the Goddess once again—and move forward in your day and into your future knowing that you have what it takes to succeed.

Blessings From Trees
Song of the Willow

Go ahead! Cry out beneath the willow tree!

Run naked under the sweep of her branches!

We will all be betrayed in one fashion or another

And shout beside the swift flowing river.

Bending over you like a mother

The willow will listen and weep.

Singing a lullaby of healing,

She will hold you in her leafy embrace.

Once loneliness has visited long enough,

You will extend your hand out to the lover yet again.

Do not fear the pain that is an inevitable part of life.

Rest beneath the willow, and then look up!

The sliver of a crescent moon

Rises as a guiding light.

Willow Ogham

196

DINDRAINE

(pronounced in French "din-drain-uh")

Dindraine In Arthurian Myth
Grail Champion

I n the 5th century, King Arthur—in a last attempt to save his kingdom Camelot from ruin—sent his knights in search of the Holy Grail. The Cup which held the blood of Christ was said to be hidden in a curious castle surrounded by a wasteland. The Grail was protected by the Fisher King, who was wounded in the thigh or groin, and awaited healing from a seeker who was pure of heart. The Fisher King has many names, but in this tale he appears as Sir Pellinore, King of Listenois. His kingdom is an island off the northwest coast of Wales, now known as Anglesey. The promise given to the knights was that the one who found the Grail would ascend to Heaven, where — like the Celtic Otherworld of Annwn — there is no hunger or disease and there is everlasting delight.

Those who are familiar with the legends of King Arthur and the Quest for the Holy Grail will know the names of Percival, Bors and Galahad, who were the three knights to receive a full vision of the sacred cup. Few know the name of the Grail heroine Dindraine, who in some early versions of the legend also received a vision of the Grail. This also would have attained her seat at Sarras, a holy isle in Arthurian legend where Grail Champions go to rest, which may also be a dimension of Heaven. Although known in France as Blanchefleur (Whiteflower), she is usually referred to as the unnamed sister of Percival. Here we restore her rightful name and her voice. It might be that Sarras is parallel in some way to the Otherworldly Tir Na Ban, the Land of Women, and that Dindraine is in the lineage of the Ladies of the Lake and the magical race of the Tuatha de Danann.

Dindɾɑine's Missing Stoɾy
A Heroine's Quest for the Holy Grail

My mother rarely spoke. It seemed that something within her was far away—as if a piece of her ran past forests and valleys and out into the ocean even as she sewed. That's how I remember her, sitting near the hearth sewing with focus and precision. The tapestries she created showed maidens with unicorns, plants, colourful flowers, sacred streams and surprising visions that never passed her lips. She was a well-behaved woman. Out of duty, she married my father, King Pellinore, and bore his children. My mother raised us well and I believe she loved us. But she was not present in this world.

One day, fearing the violent world of castles and knights, my mother fled with Percival and me into the forest. She had hoped that Percival would not see the knights in shining armor, but he did and followed them on a Quest he had to undertake. After my brother left, we returned to the castle—which I preferred. When I asked her questions, Mother would look at me as if wishing to express her truth, and then tell me that women should not ask questions but should pray. And pray I did.

The chapel was cold, but when I prayed it seemed that the stones would warm beneath my knees. I looked at the images of Mary, our Virgin Mother, and thought about the great sacrifice she had to endure with the loss of her son. My mother had also sacrificed what she held dear. Our lives as women were not like those of men. And as it was with most women, my name was not important. I was simply Percival's little sister.

When Percival came home to visit, I would rush to meet him and beg him to tell me stories of Camelot. I wanted to know all about Queen Guinevere, and I was particularly fond of my brother's quest for the Grail. Sometimes when we would sit together, a strange vision would come to me. I would see hosts of angels surrounding a cup. The luminosity of their wings made me feel faint, and when the cup spilled over, what I saw was blood. Sometimes these visions made my nose bleed or I would spit up blood. My mother observed all this, but she never said anything.

The visions would continue at night. They were splendid. Sometimes the Christ came to speak to me, but more often it was the angels. The Archangel Raphael seemed so gentle, surrounded in his pale lilac light. At other times, Archangel Michael would arrive in his blazing yellow armor. Or Gabriel would appear with his fiery trumpet. I did not share these visions with anyone.

Several suitors wooed me when it came time to marry. There was a part in my belly that wished for an earthly life. I wanted to feel a man's caress and know what it was like to be penetrated physically. It seemed to me that surrendering to someone was my calling in life. Yet something odd happened. Every time a man would get close to me, blood would begin to drip from the palms of my hands. I was embarrassed by this and tried to cover it up. The bleeding would also make me feel weak and sometimes I would faint. It was so frustrating—to lose blood and also lose the possibility of a kiss, and with it the benefits of the role of wife in hearth and home. My mother looked at me blankly; my father raged and then grew silent.

Eventually they brought a priest who asked if I wished to marry our Lord Jesus Christ. It seemed like such an odd question. I wondered how a man who was dead could be my husband, yet I had been taught not to question.

The Priest explained, "Christ has been resurrected by Spirit, so in marrying Him you would become one with God."

As he said these words, a tunnel of light opened up in the room, and then Christ stood before me in blinding light. His figure became increasingly physical, and with this new form, he radiated a soft golden hue. What I felt was the presence of a gentle man.

"Come unto me," Christ said. "You are My daughter."

His words were clear and specific. I thought everyone in the room had seen the vision, but they had not. The Priest had not seen God. I did not share my vision because I had been told that one could not see God face-to-face and live.

"I am not His bride, I am His daughter," I replied to the Priest.

The Priest looked stunned. He glanced at my mother and father, who clearly did not know what to do with me.

"She is not fit for a monastic life," the Priest sighed. Without uttering another word, he left.

From then on, as my mother and I sewed, Jesus was with me as a guiding light. I sensed him in the form of birds and in the sunlight that made its way through the castle windows. Jesus also visited me in my dreams. I knew I desired something deeply, but I wasn't sure what it was. One day, as I sat quietly looking across the green fields, He came to me holding a blazing golden chalice.

"This is what you seek," He said. "This is the cup that will quench your thirst. It is called the Grail."

That night, I mounted a horse and went in search of my brother Percival. Through the grace of Jesus, I was wrapped in a protective mist that could not be penetrated. Although I rode through wild places, I did not fear a man's touch now. I knew I would never be harmed by this world. A golden radiance opened in front of me like a pathway and I followed it for many days.

Finally I arrived with my mare at some tall castle gates. The building and the grounds had once been majestic, but were now in disrepair. The energy of the place seemed desolate, as if something were missing.

"Who goes there?" asked a man suited in armor.

"It is I, Dindraine. I am here to see my brother, Percival."

There was a long silence, and then Percival arrived at the gate on his horse and I was soon in his arms. All night he told me stories about the quests he had undertaken. I was fascinated by his adventures, yet he seemed sad. At last he could hold the news back no longer.

"I saw the Grail," he murmured with tears running down his gaunt cheeks. "I almost saved us all, but it disappeared. I have failed the Quest and my King."

I wanted to ask him so many questions, but like my mother, I knew better. I was not the one to give advice.

Suddenly I was thrown backward by a vision. As I sank to the ground, a spring rose up beneath my hands. It covered me in warm water that smelled of roses and other flowers not of this world.

"What does this mean?" asked Percival. "Are you a Lady of the Fountain?"

I did not reply, for the vision of Christ had come to me again, and the angels stood around my brother and me. Then Percival saw the vision also. His eyes grew wide, and he dropped his sword. My brother fell to his knees, humbled by the power of the Light.

"How may I redeem myself?" he asked with great humility.

The voice that responded was loud, and it echoed throughout the stone chambers of the castle. "Who does the Grail serve?"

"It serves thee," I whispered.

Percival looked at me and smiled. "It serves the Goddess," he said. "It is you I have lost."

And then I fainted.

I do not remember the next few days, for I was weak from the vision as well as a lack of food during my travels. The room I slept in was cold and grey. Sometimes I thought I saw a woman standing over me with a torch, but perhaps it was all a dream.

Once I was well, Percival explained that we had moved to the home of a Countess who suffered from leprosy. The kingdom and surrounding land depended on the health of the Countess. The woman had been told by a seer that the only way she could be healed was by drinking a cup of blood from a virgin. As my brother spoke, I felt a thrill run through my body. I knew why I had come, and that if my blood could heal the Countess, my life would not have been lived in vain.

"I am the virgin who will save the Countess, the kingdom and the land," I said knowingly.

"You are too weak," Percival replied, dismissing the idea. "You should not undertake this task. It might be too much for you and I do not want to lose you."

Despite his words, I felt more certain of doing this than anything I had ever felt before. I had no man or child, no real purpose for living beyond this task.

"Isn't loving me enough?" asked Percival. He came close, and I could feel that he was no longer a boy, but now a man. I felt his skin touch mine and something in my belly stirred.

I looked deeply into his kind brown eyes and said, "I must fulfill my Quest also, dear brother."

He lowered his gaze. A tear slipped down his left cheek, staining his armor. Percival left silently.

In the moments that followed, I felt utterly alone. My mother and father were in a distant castle and could not protect me. I did not feel the warmth of Jesus, Mary or the angels. It seemed as though the room filled with an icy wind and then a grey haze filled the air.

"Percival! Percival, where are you?" I called out, but my echoing voice was heard only by cold stones. Feeling a presence of something near me, I was filled with dread.

"Follow me," a voice in the shadows commanded. "I will show you life on Earth. You can still be a queen, my queen."

I looked through the mist at a darkly armored knight on a black horse. Although he sat still, the knight seemed to pull me towards him. I resisted.

"I am not your queen," I told the dark figure. "I am no man's queen. I am the daughter of the Christ."

He laughed.

Feeling empty, cold and frightened, I thought I might faint but knew I could not.

"There is no Christ," he contested. "The Christ is a fantasy of the priests."

I started to feel my head spinning, as if someone were trying to sever me from my own Light. "No!" I yelled. "No!" I screamed in fury. "Be gone from this place, you damned of the darkness!"

And then he was gone. I felt other ghosts and shades who pleaded for me to rescue them from their own ruin and pain. I prayed to our Savior and the Light came to me. I felt the golden radiance touch my shoulder and the love of God return to me.

Percival came into the room carrying a young woman in his arms. She had reddish hair and sores all over her body. Her eyes were swollen from crying. Her clothes were royal, but they could not hide the stench of her leprosy. A man accompanying them carried a cauldron in his left hand and a dagger in his right.

"This is the bowl that must be filled," the man said.

I looked into the woman's eyes and saw a frightened child looking back at me. My heart overflowed with compassion for her. I knew it was true that her healing would restore the land. The land and the Goddess are one. We must never forget. I was prepared to make the necessary sacrifice.

I took the dagger from the man and stuck it into my left forearm. Standing there, I felt invincible, but soon I dropped to my knees. I must have hit a major vein because the blood gushed more strongly than I thought it would. The man held the cup as it filled. With the red flow, my life force began to drain away. Percival watched as I weakened. I could sense that he wanted to stop me, but he did not. After the cup was full, Percival carried me to a seat covered in the finest material.

Resting against the back of the chair, I saw the Countess drink from the cup. Light came back into her blue eyes and her skin healed. In front of me, she became a Countess and a Goddess of the Land once again.

Seeing the healing accomplished, Percival rushed to tie a cloth around my arm to stop the flow of blood, but it did not stop. My life force flowed out of me as he wept.

It was not a bad death. In fact, it was not a death at all, because soon my friends, the angels, surrounded me and took the Light from within my body and raised it up. I hovered for a few days, listening to the prayers of Percival as he prepared a boat for my funeral. He climbed into the cold waters of the North Sea and placed my body on the oarless boat. He lit three candles and then let the candles, my body and the boat move with the current toward the island from which no one returns.

I began to send my brother a message with my thoughts. "I will see you in the holy isle of Sarras," I told him. "There we will meet again and live together forever." Percival must have heard me, for he looked skyward in my direction.

With detachment, I watched my body float past fighting and lost men. At one point, Lancelot gazed upon me, but his attention did not last long. He was still full of his own torment over his love for Guinevere. I wished to tell him it was not the Queen he sought, but the Goddess that already resided in his own heart. Perhaps Lancelot heard the message, for he knelt and wept before going off into the forest on his blind quest for the Holy Grail. I wondered when he would realize that all women are the cup.

I write this from Sarras, which is a realm of Light where those who are aligned with selfless service, love and mercy go for a time before returning. From this place, I can hear the cries of those who seek the Goddess. I even heard the quiet whispers of my mother looking for what she had lost. Mother did not come here when she died, but to some other place that souls go when they do not know how to ask the way home.

In this place, I became luminous like the angels, yet I grew increasingly sad that I had not had an experience of myself. I spoke with my counsel about my future and told them I missed the land and the clear flowing brooks. I realized that in my desire to rescue another, I had lost myself. Even my name was lost to history.

Before I fully merged with the Infinite Light, I asked that I return to Earth one more time, and that in this new life I might remember not to sacrifice myself, but to live fully and boldly. The Infinite Intelligence always grants our wishes. Immediately I could see my future-self gazing across the Pacific Ocean.

I am glad I am living in a time when a woman can touch a lover's skin without fear or judgment. I can ask questions and I can also say "no" to those who wish me to sacrifice myself for them. This is a new time, when I get to be fully me. As I walk barefoot with my future-self on the smooth sand that runs along the curling waves, I can feel my wild, unique self arising within me. And I welcome a fully lived and embodied life.

The journey is eternal, and the personal unfoldment of who I am is perfectly beautiful. Who does the Grail serve? It serves the Light within everyone.

Honoring the Heroine Dindraine

Celebrating Dindraine
Grail Knight in the Age of Light

Dindraine can be honored at the Summer Solstice, like her name-sake Aine, or any time the sun shines brightly. There is not a day in which she is specifically recognized, although we could collectively select one. My vote would be to honor Dindraine on Christmas Day. We could celebrate the Christos, the Grail Knights and all the Light Bearers who seek a healed humanity and Earth. It is time to return to the Round Table (a sacred object created in the likeness of an ouroboric circle that mirrors the shape of the Earth) and remember that all humans are created equal.

Dindraine's legend arises out of the 5th century after the demise of the Great Goddess tradition, a time in which the Christian patriarchy had disempowered the feminine and left two options for women. They were recognized either as handmaidens to salvation or the lustful daughters of Eve. During the Dark Ages, a woman could take control of her life to a certain extent by joining the ecclesiastical orders. It demanded vows of chastity, poverty and often silence.

In the tradition of the Grail legend, there were also a few more options. We discover the mysterious Ladies of the Lake, Grail Maidens and Grail Knights. A noblewoman with mystical tendencies such as Dindraine would have opted to Quest for the Holy Grail. This puts her in the lineage of the Grail Knights who actively seek mystical experiences, an archetypal role either gender can play even now. While all Grail Maidens protect the Grail for the Fisher King, not all knights need to be in service of King Arthur. Grail Knights can arise out of any culture, yet their role is always the same. They act as ethereal bridges between the spirits of the natural world and the angelic kingdoms, and serve to awaken humanity to their Divine origins.

In today's culture, we no longer need to sacrifice ourselves in the name of a higher calling. In honor of Dindraine and the Grail Knights, what we can practice daily is letting go of stories that no longer serve us. We can instead seek a higher image of ourselves, our Grail: the pure vessel that can hold the increased vibrations of the Cosmic Christos awakening in Grail Champions now.

Dindraine In Nature
Blackthorns, Hawthorns & Unicorns

The Thorn Tree is Dindraine's sacred tree. There are several varieties of thorn trees. The wood of the Blackthorn, known in the Ogham tradition as *Straif,* is generally considered a tree of challenge. The tree is tough and its long thorns can cause flesh wounds, which is perhaps why it is related to the Dark Goddess and witches. For years, it was considered unlucky, yet it has a protective energy that should be honored. Blackthorn creates natural protection in hedgerows, and in many fairytales, thorns protect a maiden while she sleeps.

The Hawthorn is a tree related to the virginal sacred feminine and her companion, the Unicorn. The thorns of the Hawthorn are shorter than the Blackthorn, but can still cause wounds. Loved by the Faery-folk, the wood of the Hawthorn, or *Huathe*, represents cleansing and purification as one prepares for literal or symbolic re-birth. White

Hawthorn blossoms remind us to actualize our spiritual gifts and the red haws invite us to take action. The Unicorn resting his head on the lap of the maiden reminds us that sexuality and spirituality are part of the fullness of life. The Thorn Trees and the Unicorn, Dindraine's magical symbols, anchor mystery and magic into our world.

Dindraine's Colours
Blue, White & Purple

Dindraine's three sacred colours are Blue, White and Purple. This triple combination is known as "Heavenly Understanding." A person who radiates Blue Light is a natural medium and is able to easily step between worlds. Yet Dindraine finds herself in the heavenly realm of Sarras before she has finished her life on Earth. Blue is also the colour of our blueprint and design, and Dindraine recognizes her error and chooses a new life in which she honors her body and understands that life is a gift that must be cherished.

A Goddess who radiates White Light has purified and cleansed herself to the point that she has integrated all the colours of the spectrum. Tears have washed away all impurities, and she becomes as enduring as a White Mountain. White is the colour that can awaken the quality of steadfastness within us.

Dindraine learns to use the colour Purple to transmute negativity and heal. Purple invites us to become aware of and transform any victim or martyr complexes that no longer serve us. Dindraine is able to work with the spiritual energies Blue, White and Purple, and evolve by gaining a holistic perspective and understanding. Dindraine can help us become aware of what we perceive in ourselves as broken, ill or missing, and learn access our own creative potential and wholeness.

Meeting the Heroine Dindraine

Dindraine learned that in order to fully know herself, she must be willing to be embodied and fully present. Life is a gift. Each one of us has a unique purpose and mission. Part of life's quest is discovering how to share yourself with the world in a way that's fulfilling to your soul. When you are ready to discover your specific qualities and capacities, call upon the Goddess Dindraine.

The Heroine's journey requires that we sacrifice ourselves to the adventure, and that we never give up hope. All High Priestesses and Ladies of the Lake learn how to use the power of the mind to part mists. It is excellent to practice, because at any moment we may be called to slip through the veil into another dimension.

217

We need to learn to still the voices of negativity and criticism. A positive mind creates a positive life. Dindraine accepts her destiny, but then chooses to live again in a way in which her wishes and dreams are satisfied. She can teach us to sacrifice what no longer serves us, so we can live our life our own way.

Practice
Developing Second Sight

One gift the Ladies of the Lake share is their ability to see not only the material world in which we live, but also the dimensions of energy that are constantly shifting and shaping our lives. In order to see with our spiritual eyes, we must learn to become very quiet and attune to the intelligence of the world around us. Second sight can seem unfamiliar, because it is not concerned with imposing our will on life. It is simply about receiving guidance from the unseen living field of intelligence that we exist within.

If you can, go and sit beside a lake or body of water. If you cannot, then imagine yourself by a lake. Notice how water changes the feeling of the landscape. Water acts as a conduit for awareness; it helps us receive messages from the living world.

Dindraine rides through the mists and then stands beside you as a guide. She touches your forehead, and suddenly sights, sounds, smells and sensations are heightened to a level you have never noticed. Take a moment to feel the many levels of existence, and how the present moment also contains both the past and the future. Knowing the future is not really different than remembering the past, because time is not linear but a circle that continues forever. The future has already happened.

Dindraine places her hand on the crown of your head. She is showing you how to read a person. Begin by sensing a family member that you dearly love. It does not matter whether they are physically close to you, on another continent, or if they have crossed on. Notice that in this moment, they are close. Just thinking about them brings their soul close to you. Take a moment and simply feel what they are feeling. You have the ability to tap into their thoughts, and send love, which will strengthen them. Look for a moment and see a year into their future. The pictures are already laid out before you, like a movie. Simply observe and then thank the Great Goddess for reminding you how to use your second sight. The more you practice, the stronger the gift will become.

Visualization
Attaining the Grail

Imagine that you are standing in a boat that is moving quietly through the mist. The pulse of your spiritual eye guides this boat to a place along the shore, a location where you intuitively know you need to land. The boat knows precisely where to go, and soon you step into a new world where trees grow with both silver and golden apples, palaces are made of crystal and brightly coloured birds sing healing songs. Feel the peace of this land, and know that your guidance has led you to the home of the Grail Castle, a dimension of Tir Na Ban, where all can be healed.

Notice that there is a Cup hovering about twelve feet in front of you that radiates Light. Realizing that this is the Holy Grail, you walk towards it with great honor and respect. Ask the Great Goddess if it is time for you to receive your Grail. If she says no, then thank her and return to this guided visualization another day.

If she responds in the affirmative, kneel before the gift that has been offered to you. You may tremble slightly, yet Dindraine's fate has already been sealed, as is your own. Ask permission to touch the Grail, and if you feel the wish is granted, then take the sacred cup into your hands. If there is liquid inside, you might wish to sip from it. Does it taste like ambrosia, the nectar of the Great Goddess? Does it have a message that is for you and you alone?

In the Otherworld, find a sacred grove, cave or a holy well where you can place your Grail for safekeeping. In your visualization, walk back to the shore and call your boat. It travels to you quickly and

221

you step into the hull. Raising your hands above your head, part the veils of the Otherworlds and arrive safely on familiar shores. Know that you may return any time you choose to this mystical place, Sarras, and that there will be other treasures and journeys awaiting your discovery.

Count slowly to three as you breathe in and feel how being in Sarras strengthened your Inner Guidance, your Body, Mind and Spirit. You need never again be disconnected from the blissful Light of spirit that loves you always. Always feel free to ask the Great Goddess questions about any area of your life, especially where you need healing.

Blessings From Trees
Song of the Hawthorn

Take my hand.

We share a dream

You and I

Of loving nights

And summer breezes.

Let's meet where

Three rivers cross

And in the shimmering

Cracks between worlds,

The swans fly south.

Let's kiss at the crossroads

With Hawthorn blossoms

In our hair, then dance

And crown the summer

King and Queen with jewels.

223

And then racing up the hill

With the shadows of the night,

Let's jump through the fires

Of our own making.

Hawthorn Ogham

APPENDIX

Eightfold Calendar
Of The Year
The Celtic Wheel of Life

The Eightfold Wheel of the Year is based on our mysterious connection to the intelligence of life. This gives us an opportunity about every six weeks to contemplate the sacred. Observing theses festivals helps us link to an ancient Earth wisdom that had been celebrated for thousands of years, which invites psychological health and wellbeing.

The Druids celebrated four solar events: *Alban Arthan* (Winter Solstice), *Alban Eilir* (Spring Equinox), *Alban Hefin* (Summer Solstice) and *Alban Elfed* (Autumn Equinox). The four lunar festivals of Beltane, Lughnasadh, Samhain and Imbolc, celebrate plants and animals.

When we choose to observe the intelligent patterns of the natural world, we can begin to move into harmony with nature. The ancient rhythms well known to our indigenous ancestors can restore health and happiness. By walking on the land and observing the life-affirming patterns of the Sun and Moon, we can learn to respond intuitively to the energies that live in each season. We can remember the creatures that live upon the Earth and acknowledge the knowing that each one carries. We can also learn to journey with the trees and begin to learn the poetic language of the Ogham.

The Celtic Wheel of Life can be used as a calendar marking the passages of the Sun and Moon. The Wheel can also be used for ceremony, for it acts as a telephone to the Otherworlds. Our prayers and messages are heard when we work with the Wheel.

If you would like to build your own Wheel, find 8 stones and, using a compass, set your stones in a place where they will not be disturbed. The more you use your Wheel the more powerful it will become. The East is known as the Gateway to new beginnings, so let's start here:*

EASTERN GATEWAY: Spring Equinox/Eostre (March 20-22): Also known as *Alban Eilir* (Light of the Earth) the Spring Equinox invites our lives to flower. Spring is in full bloom at this time, days and nights are balanced and energies are at their peak. The union of the Green Man and Mother Earth can be honored with seeds planted in prepared soil. Ancient Europeans also worshipped the Great Mother Goddess Eostre during the springtime months. Her symbol was the fertile rabbit or hare, and in some legends, she could shape-shift into a hare. Hens lay many eggs during spring and have been used for centuries to celebrate fertility and life. Eostre Eggs are often painted red in honor of the joyful Mother Goddess. Goddess Iouga can be called upon to open

---

* For more information visit the Order of Bards, Ovates & Druids: www.druidry.org

the mysteries of the Eastern Gateway and show us new ideas, lives and journeys.

SOUTHEAST GATEWAY: May Day/Beltane (April 30-May 1): The Goddess Blodeuwedd can be called upon to open the gateway of the southeast and the sensual energies of Beltane. We can honor the flower deva by reminding ourselves that we are free to choose whether to be with a lover (or not). Beltane officially begins at moonrise on April 30. Fires were traditionally lit in honor of Belenos or Bilé (the Celtic God of the Sun) and the May Queen. Once dances took place in stone circles to activate the energies of the landscape. May 1st is a day when ritual dancing is performed all over the western world in honor of the May King and Queen.

SOUTHERN GATEWAY: Summer Solstice/Litha (June 20-22): The longest day of the year – celebrated as the Summer Solstice, Litha, Midsummer, and *Alban Hefin* (the Light of Summer) – occurs at midsummer between June 20-22. Summer Solstice was witnessed as a time in which the sun stood still. Celts would light fires to add to the energy of the sun (honored as an intelligent life-sustaining force) so it could continue its cycle. This is an occasion to honor the positive qualities of the masculine and celebrate the men we know and love. Merlin, Lancelot, Galahad and other shining knights and heroes in our lives can be called upon to open the southern gateway.

SOUTHWEST GATEWAY: Lughnasadh/Lammas (July 31-Aug 1): Lleu Llaw Gyffes can be called upon to open the gateway to the harvest time of Lughnasadh, which means the games of Lugh (a Celtic Sun God). In myth and legend, it is said that the Goddess Taillte once resided on the magical *Temair* (Hill of Tara). In ancient Ireland, she was known as the foster-mother of the Light, who took in the embodied form as the Sun God, Lugh. Upon her death, she requested that games be held each year in her honor on the lands she had cleared. Lugh held the first games, which were rather like an early Irish Olympics. There was also music, feasting and storytelling. Today many people make a meal to celebrate the harvest and the feminine energy that sustains us.

WESTERN GATEWAY: Autumn Equinox/Mabon (September 21-22): Elaine and the Ladies of the Lake can open the gateway of the west and swim with the wise salmon to the Otherworlds. Mabon is a time to rest after the harvest, and is symbolized by the Cornucopia or the Horn of Plenty – both a masculine and feminine symbol. On *Alban Elfed* (the Light of Water) the days and nights are equally balanced. This is a time to give thanks to the goodness of the Great Goddess who nourishes us. The Ladies of the Lake remind us that although we are constantly changing forms, our essence never dies.

NORTHWEST GATEWAY: Samhain (October 31– November 2): The reign of the Winter Queen begins at this time. On these three days, the veils between our world and the Otherworlds are thin. It is a time to honor our ancestors and guardians who have supported us throughout our lives. Elen Luyddog, the Lady of the Wildwood, is the Goddess who can open the northwest gateway. She is a master shape-shifter and knows when it is time to release what no longer serves us and also knows how to dance with shades and spirits.

NORTHERN GATEWAY: Winter Solstice/Yule (Dec 20-22): *Alban Arthan* (the Light of Arthur) is the time to honor our ancestors, and acknowledge the natural cycle of death and rebirth. The darkness of winter is cast off and the promise of spring and summer returns. A Yule log is prepared with leaves, along with messages of what is outdated, and families gather to invite in the Light of the new sun. Arianrhod can be celebrated during the Winter Solstice, the shortest day of the year. A silver star can be hung indoors in honor of Arianrhod and her magical Silver Circle.

NORTHEASTERN GATEWAY: Imbolc (February 1-2): The return of light and life is celebrated during this Lunar festival. Imbolc marks the ending of winter when lambs are born and the first flowers begin to appear. Fires are lit to awaken the Goddess Brighid; stories are told and snowdrops are planted in her honor. We can also honor the Grail Champion Dindraine who opened the gates to Sarras, a realm of paradise.

Glossary

A Brief Dictionary of Celtic Myth
& Arthurian Legend

Alban Arthan: (Welsh for "Light of Winter" or "Light of Arthur") **Winter Solstice** is the darkest time of the year. It is the time of year when the Sun dies and is reborn, symbolized by King Arthur. See: **Yule.**

Alban Eilir: ("Light of the Earth") the name used by Druids for the festival of the **Spring Equinox,** a time of balance and new life. See: **Ostara.**

Alban Elfed: ("Light of Water") the name used by Druids for the festival or feast of the **Autumn Equinox.** See: **Mabon.**

Alban Hefin ("Light of the Shore" or "Light of Summer")**: Summer Solstice** in the **Druid** tradition. Midsummer is celebrated annually around June 21, the longest day of the year. See: **Litha.**

Albion: the oldest known name for the island of Britain; the original blueprint or soul of Britain and Ireland, and perhaps the soul of the earth. The Celtic name for Scotland was Alba.

Amfortas: the **Fisher King** of **Castle Corbenic** (or **Carbonek**), and the descendent of **Joseph of Arimathea** whose role is to guard the Holy Grail, the Cup from the Last Supper.

Annwn (Welsh pronunciation "Ah-noon"): the Celtic Underworld of eternal youth and delights ruled by Arawn or **Gwyn ap Nudd**. In Christianity, it is the equivalent of a realm of Heaven. The Druids spoke of Annwn as the Abyss, a place where the soul-force abides. According to Welsh Bards, the soul begins in **Annwn,** lives in the material world of Abred, then when embracing love, goodness and light, rises to Gwynvyd, a circle of immortal beings. The final circle of Ceugant is reserved for God alone. Finding these circles is part of the Grail quest.

Anu: Celtic Goddess of Fertility. An Irish Mother-Goddess. See: **Danu** and **Don.**

Argante: one of the nine Ladies of the Lake, often said to be the foster mother of **Lancelot.** She may also be a guardian of **Elaine** and **Galahad.**

Arianrhod (Welsh pronunciation "Ahr-ee-AHN-hrod"): Welsh heroine or Goddess.

Arthur: a hero of Britain who rode into **Annwn** and seized a cauldron or grail. This quest becomes a journey of secrets and magic, a quest for the grail. See: **King Arthur.**

Athena: Greek Goddess of Wisdom, Warfare and Civilization. See: **Minerva** and **Brigantia. Autumn Equinox**: see **Mabon.**

Avalon: the Otherworldly dimension with portals in Glastonbury; the same or similar to **Tir Na Ban,** the Land of Women.

Avebury: Neolithic and Bronze Age stone circle and henge built between 2850 BCE and 2200 BCE in South West England. Similar to Stonehenge, it is another British megalithic monument. Mystics claim it is the energetic umbilicus of Earth created when our planet was formed.

Belenos (known in Welsh as "Beli Mawr"): Celtic God of the Sun and consort of Anu. His festival is **Beltane**, when bonfires are lit to welcome in summer. He was absorbed into Christianity as St. George. In Arthurian legend, he becomes Sir King **Pellinore** of Listenois.

Beli or Beli Mawr (see **Belenos** and **Bilé**): consort to the Welsh Mother Goddess, Don, and father of **Arianrhod**.

Beltane: Celtic May Day, beginning at moonrise on May Day Eve, it is traditionally celebrated on May 1. The Spring fertility festival honors the solar divinity **Beli** or **Belenos** and his union with the **May Queen**. Weddings and hand-fastings are common at this time. It is often celebrated with May Pole dancing and jumping the Beltane fires for luck. For the Celts, it was a day when people (married or unmarried) chose partners to make love with.

Bilé (pronunciation "billie"): Celtic God of Light and Healing and the consort of **Danu** or **Don**. His name means sacred tree and his main festival is **Beltane**.

Blodeuwedd (Welsh pronunciation "blod-u-with"): a Goddess created out of leaves and flowers. She was the wife of **Lleu Llaw Gyffes** and became the lover of **Gronw Pebr**, who attempted to kill Lleu. As a punishment for her crimes, she was turned into an owl.

Boann: the Irish Goddess of Wisdom and white cows. The wife of **Elcmar**, lover of the **Dagda** and mother of **Aengus**. Also known as the Irish Goddess of the River Boyne, and a sister Goddess of **Iouga**.

Bors de Ganis: from Arthurian legend, he was one of three knights of the **Round Table** to achieve the **Grail**.

Brigantes: a pre-Roman Celtic tribe who resided in Northern Britain.

Brigantia: Goddess of the **Brigantes,** also known as the high or exalted one. She corresponds to the Irish Goddess **Brighid.** She has been linked to the Roman Goddess **Minerva** and the Greek Goddess **Athena.**

Brighid, Brigid, or Brigit: Goddess who was absorbed into Celtic Christianity as St. Brigit. In Britain, she is known as **Brigantia,** patron Goddess of the **Brigantes.**

Caer Sidi: an Otherworldly island and home of the Goddess **Arianrhod.**

Camelot: the legendary court of **King Arthur**, which may now be Cadbury Camp in Somerset. Camelot was an ideal kingdom where knights gathered around the **Round Table**, a symbol of unity.

Candlemas: a Christian holiday celebrated February 2. See **Imbolc.**

Carbonek: (See: **Castle Corbenic.**)

Castle Corbenic (or **Carbonek**): the Grail Castle and home of the lineage of **Fisher Kings** in Arthurian mythology and in some versions, **Elaine.** It could appear to be mundane, but was full of adventurous items for Grail seekers, such as dragons and boiling cauldrons. It was also said to be the birthplace of **Galahad.**

Cauldron of Annwn: the Grail, which was later Christianized into the Holy Grail.

cauldrons: in Celtic mythology, there are many, including **Dadga**'s Cauldron of Abundance, **Ceridwen**'s Cauldron of Wisdom, and King Bran's Cauldron of Rebirth (*Pair Dadeni).* See **Grail.**

Ceridwen or **Keridwen**: Welsh Goddess of Wisdom. She is sometimes referred to the old White One who possessed a cauldron that becomes known as the Grail.

Cernunnos: (pronounced "ker-nun-nous") the most ancient and perhaps the greatest of Celtic Gods. He is usually depicted with antlers and called the horned one. The Celts believed horns were related to male potency, but the symbolism was misunderstood and demonized by the Christian church. See: **Gwyn Ap Nudd.**

Chalice Well: one of Britain's most ancient wells located in the valley of **Avalon** in Somerset at the base of a sacred hill known as the Glastonbury Tor. In folklore, it is said that the well opened in the earth when the Holy Grail (the Cup or Chalice used at the Last Supper) was placed there by **Joseph of Arimathea**. It is more likely that it was built by the old **Druids**. The well is said to have magical powers, perhaps even to provide a bridge to the Afterlife.

Constantine: also known as Constantine "the Blessed," or Custennin Fendigaid, was the son of **Mascen Wledig** and **Elen Lwyddog**. Some historians credit him with the Christianization of the Roman Empire. In Geoffrey's *Historia Regum Britanniae,* Constantine is **King Arthur's** kinsman and succeeds him as King of Britain.

Dagda: God of Goodness, Abundance and Fertility.

Danu: Celtic Goddess, known in Ireland as the Mother of the Tuatha Dé Danann. In Welsh mythology, she is known as Don. In Arthurian Legend, the daughters in her ancient lineage tend to have *aine* in their names, such as Elaine and Dindraine. See: **Anu** and **Don.**

deva: a nature spirit or spiritual force within nature.

Dindraine (pronounced in French "Din-drain-uh"): The daughter of King **Pellinore** and the sister of **Percival**, Dindraine is called on the Grail Quest. As a descendent of **Joseph of Arimathea**, she was drawn to the quest and eventually became a Grail Champion.

Don (known in Ireland as **Danu** or **Anu**): Welsh Mother-Goddess.

dragon: a mythological beast and a symbol of the Goddess; usually linked in mythology with the Grail codes.

Druids: the name is derived from the Celtic words "dru" meaning tree and "wid" meaning to know. Trees have always been respected by the Druids, learned people of the Celts who have a history dating back at least 25,000 years. The Druids were the respected wise men and women who lived amongst the ancient Celts in the landscape of Ireland, Britain and Gaul (western France). It is thought that Druids believed in reincarnation and practiced spiritual re-birth in caves to awaken creative powers. Although accused of human sacrifice (which the warring Celts practiced), it is now widely believed that the Druids were not generally violent, but focused on astrology, poetry, philosophy and spirituality, training up to twenty years. There is currently a strong Neo-Druid revival.

Dylan Ail Don: Son of **Arianrhod**, known as Son of Wave. He is the power of darkness, while his brother **Lleu** is the power of Light.

Elaine: one of the Ladies of the Lake, and mother (with Lancelot) of the Grail Champion **Galahad**. Her father was **Amfortas, the Fisher King** of **Castle Corbenic**, a descendent of **Joseph of Arimathea**, Guardian of the Cup from the Last Supper. She may also be in the lineage of the Goddess **Aine/Anu**.

Elen: also known as "Elen of the Ways," she is a Goddess of Sovereignty who can act as a guide during times of change. The Lady of the Wildwood has been worshipped since Paleolithic times. Elen is linked to fertility and the wellbeing of the land. She is generally depicted with antlers. See: **Elen Luyddog.**

Elen Luyddog: Lwydogg in Welsh means "of the Hosts." **Elen** was a semi-historical Welsh woman who is said to have lived from 340 to 388 AD. She is also known as **Saint Helena of Caernarfon,**

and was said to have ordered the building of Sarn Helen, a great Roman road that runs through Wales. She was the wife of **Magnus Maximus**, a Spanish-born Roman Emperor, who was absorbed into Welsh mythology as **Mascen Wledig.** In some versions of Arthurian legend, she is related to **King Arthur.** (Also see **Saint Elen.**)

Elohim: a group of angelic beings who love and care for the earth. From Biblical Hebrew, the plural noun for Gods until the rise of monotheism in 2 CE.

Faery: comes from the French word "faerie." Faeries are generally connected with the elemental forces of nature, and they are considered to have magical powers. Those of the Faery Faith (the Gaelic term) are described as beautiful and immortal, and sometimes dangerous. In Wales, the Faery-folk are known as the **Tylwyth Teg.**

familiar, familiar spirit or **personal totem**: an animal, animal guide or supernatural being that assists magical people. Familiars are popular in myths and fairy tales.

Fisher King or the **Wounded King**: a lineage of kings who are the Guardians of the Holy Grail. The Fisher King has usually been wounded in the thigh, groin or genitals, which makes him impotent. His suffering creates a Wasteland. In some tales, his name is **Amfortas** or **King Pelles**, other names include King **Pellinore**. His castle is generally **Carbonek**, a place of strange adventures, but all he is able to do is fish and wait for the Grail knight who will achieve the Grail and heal the land. **Percival, Dindraine**, Bors and **Galahad** are all Grail achievers. The Fisher King may be related to the older God **Belenos** or **Beli Mawr,** who was absorbed into Christianity as St. George.

Galahad: a Grail winner in Arthurian legend. Son of **Lancelot** and **Elaine, Galahad** was born at **Castle Corbenic,** home of the **Fisher King**.

Geis, geas **or** *geasa*: an idiosyncratic taboo, curse, spell, obligation or prohibition placed upon someone. The Scottish Gaelic spelling is "geas." It has to do with the contracts made by the soul.

Gilfaethwy (Welsh pronunciation "Gil-VAY-thooee" — "gil" as in the gills on a fish): **Arianrhod**'s violent brother who raped **Goewin**.

Glastonbury: a town in southwestern England recognized as a spiritual center since the megalithic era. A five-thousand-year-old astrological wheel is carved into the landscape. It has long been recognized as the heart chakra of the Earth. Legend has it that after the resurrection of Christ, **Joseph of Arimathea** brought the Holy Grail with him and shifted the energy of Jerusalem to Glastonbury. Lady Chapel was built in the center of the spiritual vortex. Glastonbury is the **Avalon** of Arthurian legend and the site of the first Christian church in England.

Glastonbury Abbey: a monastery in Glastonbury, Somerset, England founded in the 7th century, although some say it was built by **Joseph of Arimathea** and the boy Jesus in the 1st century. Since the 12th century, it has been associated with the legends of **King Arthur**.

Glastonbury Tor: the Celtic name for the Tor is "Ynys Gutrin," which means Isle of Glass. Thousands of years ago, it was an island. The **Druids** used the Tor from 2500 BCE and still consider it to be their spiritual center. The roofless St. Michael's Tower stands at the top of the hill, and people from all around the world make pilgrimages to the sacred site. The Tor is associated with **Avalon, Annwn** and the myths of **King Arthur**.

glefiosa (Welsh pronunciation "glay fee'sa"): Welsh term for the Light of Inner Wisdom, also known as the bright knowledge which is often granted from the Otherworld.

Goddess: female deities that appear in polytheistic religions, including the ancient Egyptians, Romans, Greeks and Celts. In some traditions there is also a monotheistic Great Goddess or Earth Mother. Feminists have turned to the Goddess in an attempt to discover the feminine face of God/Goddess, which is missing in Judeo-Christian theology.

Goddess of Sovereignty: She appears in Arthurian legend as the **Loathy Lady**, who could be transformed by a kiss into a beautiful maiden. In Celtic mythology, she is the bride of the king who must be fertile and rule wisely or forfeit his reign to a younger king.

Goewin: the virgin foot-holder for King Math (**Math fab Mathonwy**).

Grail or **Holy Grail**: in Arthurian legend, the Grail is the cup or platter that Jesus used at the Last Supper, or the cup in which the blood of Christ was collected at the crucifixion. After the resurrection, Joseph of Arimathea took the cup through France to Britain. Some say the Grail was Mary Magdalene and her daughters. The Grail has deeper roots in Celtic mythology, appearing as the **Dagda**'s Cauldron of Abundance, Ceridwen's Cauldron of Wisdom and King Bran's Cauldron of Rebirth, amongst others.

Grail Castle: (See: **Castle Corbenic.**)

Green Man: a nature Deity, sometimes referred to as the May King. He is generally shown with a face made of leaves and is a symbol of re-birth. His partner is the Green Lady.

Gronw Pebr: the Lord of Penllyn, he is a warrior, hunter and lover of **Blodeuwedd**. In some versions of the myth, he murders **Lleu Llaw Gyffes**.

Guinevere: the beautiful **May Queen** and wife of **King Arthur**. Her dowry was the **Round Table**, the focus of **Camelot**. After the 12th century, she becomes ensnared in a love triangle with **Lancelot**. Guinevere may have been based on historical Eleanor of Aquitaine, the powerful 12th century Queen of France and then England, who loved Arthurian legends and helped spread their popularity.

Gwydion (Welsh pronunciation "GWID-ee-yon"): **Arianrhod**'s brother and the father of **Lleu Llaw Gyffes**. Means trees or forest in Welsh.

Gwyn ap Nudd (Welsh pronunciation "gwin ap nead"): Son of Nudd, he originally comes from Welsh folklore where he is known as the king of the **Tylwyth Teg** or Faery realm and ruler of the Welsh Otherworld, known as **Annwn**. He is often depicted as a warrior with a blackened face and the leader of the Wild Hunt, who rides through the skies on rainy autumn nights. Mystics say he lives in the hollow hill of Glastonbury Tor. His name means white or holy. He is sometimes connected to the more frightening antlered **Herne the Hunter.**

hand-fasting: a Celtic wedding ceremony.

henge: a prehistoric circular earthwork, usually with standing stones.

Herne the Hunter: a figure from British folklore who is said to live in Windsor Forest. A horned spirit who may be a woodland Deity, a **Green Man**, or a version of the ancient Celtic God **Cernunnos**. See: **Gwyn Ap Nudd.**

Historia Regum Britanniae: also known as *The History of the Kings of Britain*, this historical collection was written around 1136 by Geoffrey of Monmouth. The book chronicles two thousand years of British kings and was acclaimed as a true history until the 16th century, but is now considered fictitious.

Holy Grail: (See: **Grail**.)

Igraine: mother of King Arthur, and another Lady of the Lake.

Imbolc (Gaelic pronunciation "IM-bulk" or "ee-Molk"): also known as **Candlemas** or Bride's Day, an ancient ceremony held on February 1 or 2 of each year in honor of the Goddess **Brighid**). It is one of the four Celtic fire ceremonies and marks the passage of winter into spring. Imbolc honors the phases of the triple Goddess: maiden, mother and crone.

Iouga: a Proto-Celtic Goddess worshipped in York, England. Her exact name is unknown. She may be a reminder of the Goddesses from pre-Christian Iona.

Isle of Avalon: (See: **Avalon**.)

Joseph of Arimathea: a biblical and Arthurian hero who buried Jesus after the crucifixion on Mount Golgotha, the mountain of the skull. In early Christian lore, it is said that he took the cup or Holy Grail that had held the blood of Jesus around the Mediterranean converting people to Christianity. He eventually settled in **Glastonbury.** When he thrust his staff into the ground on Wearyall Hill, it blossomed into a tree known as the Holy Thorn. A piece of the tree is still growing in the Chalice Well gardens. It was supposedly Joseph who built the first church in England.

King Arthur: an historic early Celtic king or warrior named Arthur existed in the 5th century. The tales of King Arthur are largely mythological. The first legend was originally recorded in 6th century Wales, and the stories were made popular in the 12th century by British writer Geoffrey of Monmouth and the French poet Chretien de Troyes. In short, Arthur, son of Uther Pendragon and the deceived Queen Igraine, was snatched away at birth by **Merlin** and raised to be King of **Camelot**. Sir Thomas Malory, Alfred Tennyson, T. H. White and other writers have added to the tales, which continue to inspire writers and spiritual seekers today. It is said that Arthur never died but was taken to **Avalon** where he is becoming the once and future king.

Kundry: a **Lady of the Lake** and Goddess of Sovereignty, who could appear as a beautiful maiden or as a hag.

Lady of the Lake or the **Ladies of the Lake**: an Otherworldly Goddess (or several Goddesses) who sometimes empowers humans so they can work for the greater good. In Arthurian legend, the Lady of the Lake has at least ten names and faces, returning always in new forms. Lady of the Lake is an eternal Goddess of Sovereignty, whose work is to heal the land. Perhaps when the time is right, she will awaken **Merlin** and usher in a new Renaissance of Light.

Lammas (see: **Lughnasadh**): A celebration on August 1 in honor of the Sun God Lugh. The Greek Goddesses Demeter and Ceres are also honored at this time.

Lancelot: a knight in Arthurian legend, lover of Queen **Guinevere** and **Elaine**, and father of **Galahad**.

Listenois: another name for the Grail Kingdom. It is the strange land that surrounds **Castle Corbenic.** When the **Fisher King** is injured, it is known as the Wasteland.

Litha: also known as Midsummer, **Summer Solstice** and **Alban Hefin** ("Light of Summer" or "Light of the Shore") is celebrated annually around June 21, the longest day of the year. It is considered the most powerful day for both the sun's and the Sun God's or Goddess's full power.

Lleu Llaw Gyffes (Welsh pronunciation "Lei lau gefe-sis"): **Arianrhod** and **Gwydion**'s son and hero of Welsh mythology. Lleu means Light. See: **Lugh** and **Lughnasadh.**

Loathy Lady: a woman who appears ugly (unattractive, *loathly*), but who transforms when a man loves her regardless of her appearance. A Loathy Lady can become the most beautiful and desirable of all women. It is then revealed that her ugliness was the result of a curse, which was broken by the hero's action.

Lugh (Irish pronunciation "Loo"): a son of the **Dagda** in Irish Mythology, who ruled as an Irish High King. Lugh was known for the brightness of his face, as well as his many skills. He led the **Tuatha Dé Danann** in a victory over the **Formorians**. His Welsh counterpart is **Lleu Llaw Gyffes.**

Lughnasadh/Lughnasa (also known as **Lammas**): named after the sun god, **Lugh**. The festival is celebrated on August 1, which marks the ending of the Celtic year. Lughnasadh is the last of the four great feasts (the Celtic year begins with **Samhain** on October 31/November 1). In Ireland, it is said that **Lugh** created the festival in honor of the Earth Goddess Tailtui.

Mabinogion (Welsh pronunciation "mab-in-O-gee-on") **or** *Mabinogi*: a collection of Welsh stories from the 14th century.

Mabon: a Celtic festival of mid-harvest, celebrated on **Autumn Equinox**, around September 21. It also known as **Alban Elfed** (the Light of Water).

Magnus Maximus: (See: **Mascen Wledig**.)

Mascen Wledig (Welsh pronunciation "Maxen Le-dig"): the Welsh name for **Magnus Maximus**, a western Roman Emperor who lived from approximately 335-388 AD. He was married to **Elen** who became known as **Elen Lwyddog "of the Hosts" of Britain**, and later **Saint Helena**. Their son was known as **Custennin Fendigaid Constantine "the Blessed."** In some tales, he was the father of **Ambrosius** (father of **Merlin**) and **Uther Pendragon** (father of **King Arthur**) who defended Britain against the invading Saxon.

Math fab Mathonwy or **Mathonwy of Gwynnedd** or **King Math**: the shadowy magician King who fooled Arianrhod.

May Queen: the fertile Maiden of earth selected to represent the continuation of life. When she is happy, the landscape flourishes. Her holiday is **Beltane. Guinevere** and **Brighid** are both celebrated as **May Queens**. The May Queen's consort is the May King, **Green Man**, or the horned God **Herne the Hunter**. His older version is **Cernunnos**. They unite in a sacred marriage of the Earth and the sun.

Melyngan Mangre: Lleu Llaw Gyffes' faithful golden chestnut horse.

Merlin or Merlyn: ancient wizard, **Druid** and wise magician featured in Arthurian legend as **King Arthur's** guide and mentor. Some mythologists say Merlin and the **Elohim** are star beings that co-created the template of **Albion**, the soul of the living Earth.

Minerva: the Roman Goddess of Wisdom, Art and Warfare. She is linked to the Greek Goddess **Athena.** See: **Brigantia**.

Morgan le Fey or Morgana: Queen of Avalon, she is paradoxically a Priestess, healer and a dark magician.

Nimue or **Nymue** (Cornish pronunciation "nim-we"): one of the nine **Ladies of the Lake.** The lover, student and sometimes nemesis of **Merlin.**

Ostara (Spring Equinox): the original Easter, when eggs are painted and flowers are gathered. It is celebrated around March 21. See: **Alban Eilir.**

Pair Dadeni: the Cauldron of Rebirth. See: **Grail.**

Pellinore: the King of Listenois (possibly Anglesey, an island off the coast of Wales) was said to be in the lineage of **Joseph of Arimathea.** His descendants are charged with the responsibility of guarding the Holy Grail. He is the son of King Pellam and brother of Kings Pelles and Alain. Sir Pellinore is best known for fighting with Arthur and breaking the sword pulled from the stone. He has many children including **Dindraine** and **Percival.** His grandnephew is Grail Champion **Galahad.** He may be connected to the older God **Belenos** and later St. George.

Percival, Parsifal or **Parzifal**: an Arthurian hero first written about in 1175. He is the German Parzival who appears in Wagner's 19th century opera. His name arises from the Persian "Fal Parsi" which means pure fool. Percival is a Grail Champion in Arthurian legend, and brother of **Dindraine.** Although he failed in his first attempt, Percival found the Grail Castle again and he asked why the lance bled, which healed the **Fisher King** and allowed the land to flourish once more. In some legends, he is also the brother of **Elaine.**

Round Table: a table built in the Otherworld, which symbolized unity and spiritual brotherhood.

Saint Brigit: a holy woman of the Celtic Church, linked with the Goddess **Brighid** or **Brigid.**

Saint Elen or Helena: The ancient Goddess **Elen** was absorbed into Christianity as Helena. Saint Helena founded churches in 4th century Wales. Many holy wells throughout Britain are dedicated to her. In some version of Arthurian legend, she is related to **King Arthur**.

Saint Helena of Caernarfon: She was said to have ordered the building of Sarn Helen, a great Roman road that runs through Wales. Saint Helena is the patron saint of British road builders. (See: **Saint Elen**.)

Samhain (Gaelic pronunciation "Sah-win"; some Irish speakers say "Shavnah"): Halloween, All Hallow's Eve or Samhain is celebrated around October 31. Marking the end of the Celtic year, it is a time to honor the ancestors and think of those who have passed away.

Sarras: a holy isle in Arthurian legend where **Grail** champions go to rest.

Sidhe (Irish pronunciation "Shee"): the tall beautiful people of myth and legend.

Solas Siorai (Irish pronunciation "solace sherry"): Gaelic term meaning "eternal light."

sylph: elemental being connected with air, often called a **Faery.**

Summer Solstice: (See: **Litha** and **Alban Hefin**)

Tir Na Ban or **Tir Na mBan** (Irish pronunciation "Tir na Ban"): a legendary Otherworldly land of women. See **Avalon**.

Tuatha Dé Danann or simply **Tuatha Dé** or **Tuatha** (Irish pronunciation "Too-a-ha-dae Donnan"): Tribe of the Goddess Danu, a supernatural race in Celtic mythology.

Tylwyth Teg: in Welsh lore, they are small child-like beings or Faery-folk who live in lakes or underground. Their king was known as **Gwyn Ap Nudd.** Also known as the fair-folk, they generally wore blue clothes. They are attracted to toadstools and have a mixed reputation.

undines: elemental beings associated with water.

Uther Pendragon: King Uther is the father of **King Arthur.**

Winter Solstice: (See **Yule** and **Alban Arthan**)

Yule: arising out of the Anglo-Saxon word "Iul," — it means wheel. It is a celebration of the Wheel of Life. Yule is observed on the **Winter Solstice,** around December 21, the shortest day of the year. One of the four Fire Ceremonies of the Celts, it is hailed as the time when the Goddess becomes the Great Mother and gives birth to the Sun King. Yule was absorbed into Christianity as Christmas. Mystics know that in the darkest of times, it is wise to seek a spark of hope and ask for the return of Light. It is a day to honor the feminine and all of the women in your life. (See: **Alban Arthan**)

Bibliography

Blair, Nancy. *The Book of Goddesses*, Vega, London, England, 2002.

Bolen, Jean Shinoda, MD. *Goddesses in Everywoman: Powerful Archetypes in Women's Lives,* Harper Perennial, New York, NY, 1984.

Bonheim, Jalaja, editor. *Goddess: A Celebration in Art and Literature,* Stewart, Tabori & Chang: New York, NY, 1997.

Caldecott, Morya. *Women in Celtic Myth,* Arrow Books, London, England, 1988.

Campbell, Joseph. *Goddesses: Mysteries of the Feminine Divine,* New World Library, Novato, CA, 2013.

Cates, Ayn Wesley. *Disguise, Deceit and the Divine Spokesperson: A Study of Lady Gregory's Plays,* Doctoral Thesis approved by King's College London, April 1993. (Interlibrary Loan: Senate House, London, England, UK)

Coghlan, Ronan. *The Illustrated Encyclopedia of Arthurian Legends*, Barnes & Noble Books, New York, NY, 1995.

Downing, Christine. *Women's Mysteries, Toward a Poetics of Gender,* Spring Journal, Inc., New Orleans, LA, 2003.

Ellis, Peter Berresford. *The Druids,* William B. Eerdman's Publishing Co., Grand Rapids, MI, 1994.

Gimbutas, Marija. *The Goddesses and Gods of Old Europe, Myths and Cult Images,* University of California Press, Berkeley and Los Angeles, CA, 2007.

Gimbutas, Marija. *The Living Goddesses,* University of California Press, Berkeley and Los Angeles, CA, 1999.

Godwin, Malcolm. *The Holy Grail: Its Origins, Secrets, and Meaning Revealed,* Barnes & Noble Books, New York, NY, 1998.

Graves, Robert. *The White Goddess: A Historical Grammar of Poetic Myth,* Farrar, Straus and Giroux, New York, NY, 2013.

Green, Roger Lancelyn. *King Arthur and His Knights of the Round Table,* Puffin Books/Penguin, London & NY, 1953/2008.

Gregory, Lady. *Gods and Fighting Men,* Colin Smythe, Gerrards Cross, Buckinghamshire, England, 1905/1970.

Guest, Lady C. (editor & translator). *The Mabinogion,* Ballantyne Press, London, England, 1910.

Harte, Jeremy. *English Holy Wells: A Sourcebook,* Heart of Albion Press, Avebury, England, 2008.

Hidalgo, Sharlyn. *Celtic Tree Oracle,* Blue Angel Publishing, Victoria, Australia, 2017.

Hidalgo, Sharlyn. *The Healing Power of Trees,* Llewellyn Publications, Woodbury, MN, 2015.

Hoffman, Mary. *Women of Camelot: Queens and Enchantresses at the Court of King Arthur,* Abbeville Press, NY, 2000.

Hogan, Timothy. "The Way of the Templar: A Manual for the Modern Knight Templar, Chevalier Emerys, Grand Master Ordre Souverain du Temple Initiatique," Manual of CIRCES International, 2015.

Jones, Kathy. *The Ancient British Goddess: Her Myths, Legends, Sacred Sites and Present Day Revelation,* Ariadne Publications, Glastonbury, England, 2001.

Jones, Kathy. *Priestess of Avalon, Priestess of the Goddess: A Renewed Spiritual Path for the 21ˢᵗ Century,* Ariadne Publications, Glastonbury, England, 2006.

Jones, Kathy. *Spinning the Wheel of Ana: A Spiritual Quest to Find the British Primal Ancestors,* Ariadne Publications, Glastonbury, England, 1994.

Lacy, Norris J., Geoffrey Ashe, and Debra N. Mancoff. *The Arthurian Handbook, Second Edition,* Routledge, New York, NY, 2013.

Leitch, Yuri. *Gwyn: Ancient God of Glastonbury and key to the Glastonbury Zodiac,* Temple Publications, Somerset, UK, 2007.

Leviton, Richard. *Looking for Arthur: A Once and Future Travelogue,* Station Hill Openings/Barrytown Ltd., Barrytown, NY, 1997.

Loomis, Roger Sherman. *The Grail: From Celtic Myth to Christian Symbol,* Constable and Company Limited, London, England, 1992.

Malory, Sir T. *Le Morte d'Arthur.* (Editor John Matthews) Orion, London, England, 2000.

Markale, Jean. *Women of the Celts,* Inner Traditions, Rochester, VT, 1972.

Matthews, Caitlin. *King Arthur and the Goddess of the Land: The Divine Feminine in the Mabinogion,* Inner Traditions, Rochester, VT, 2002.

Matthews, Caitlin. *Celtic Visions: Seers, Omens and Dreams of the Otherworld,* Watkins Publishing, London, England, 2012.

Matthews, Caitlin and John. *Ladies of the Lake,* Aquarian Press, London, England, 1992.

Matthews, John. *The Celtic Reader: Selections from Celtic Legend, Scholarship and Story,* Aquarian Press, London, UK, 1992.

Matthews, John. *The Celtic Shaman: A Practical Guide,* Rider/Penguin Random House Group, London, England, 1991/2001.

McCoy, Edain. *Celtic Women's Spirituality: Accessing the Cauldron of Life,* Llewellyn Publications, Woodbury, MN, 1998.

Monaghan, Patricia, Ph.D. *The Encyclopedia of Celtic Mythology and Folklore,* Checkmark Books, New York, NY, 2008.

Monaghan, Patricia, Ph.D. *Encyclopedia of Goddesses and Heroines,* New World Library, Novato, CA, 2014.

Monaghan, Patricia, Ph.D. *The Goddess Companion: Daily Meditations on the Feminine Spirit,* Llewellyn Publications, Woodbury, MN, 1999.

Monaghan, Patricia, Ph.D. *The Goddess Path: Myths, Invocations, and Rituals,* Llewellyn Publications, Woodbury, MN, 1999.

Monmouth, Geoffrey of. *History of the Kings of Britain,* Harmondsworth, Penguin, 1984.

Moorey, Teresa. *The Magic and Mystery of Trees,* Capall Bann Publishing, Somerset, England, 2006.

Morgan, Giles. *A Brief History of The Holy Grail: History, Myth, Religion,* Running Press Book Publishers, Philadelphia, PA, 2011.

O'Donohue, John. *Benedictus: A Book of Blessings*, Bantam Press, London, England, 2007.

Peters, June & Bernard Kelly. *The Seat Perilous: Arthur's Knights and the Ladies of the Lake*, The History Press, Gloucestershire, England, 2013.

Rankine, David and Sorita D'Este. *The Isles of the Many Gods,* Avalonia, London, England, 2007.

Spence, Lewis. *Mysteries of Celtic Britain,* Parragon, Bristol, England, 1998.

Steiner, Rudolf. *Christ and the Spiritual World: And the Search for the Holy Grail*, Rudolf Steiner Press, East Sussex, England, 2008.

Stewart, R.J. *Celtic Myths, Celtic Legends,* Blandford Press, London, England, 1996.

Stewart, R.J. *Merlin and Woman: The Book of the Second Merlin Conference,* Blandford Press, London, England, 1988.

Sykes, Brian. *Blood of the Isles: Exploring the genetic roots of our tribal history,* Transworld Publishers: Corgi edition, Great Britain, 2007.

Sykes, Brian. *Saxons, Vikings and Celts: The Genetic Roots of Britain and Ireland,* W.W. Norton & Co., New York and London, 2006.

Troyes, Chretien de. *Arthurian Romances.* Translated by William W. Kibler, Penguin Books, London, England, 1991.

Waite, Arthur Edward. *The Vulgate Cycle of the Holy Grail,* Kessinger Publishing, 2005.

Weir, Alison. *Eleanor of Aquitaine*, Ballantine/Random House, New York, NY, 1999.

Wilde, Lyn Webster. *Celtic Inspirations: Essential Meditations and Texts,* Duncan Baird Publishers, London, England, 2004.

Wilde, Lyn Webster. *Celtic Women: In Legend, Myth and History,* Cassell, London England, 1997.

Wise, Caroline (editor). *Finding Elen: The Quest for Elen of the Ways,* Eala Press, London, England, 2015.

Notes